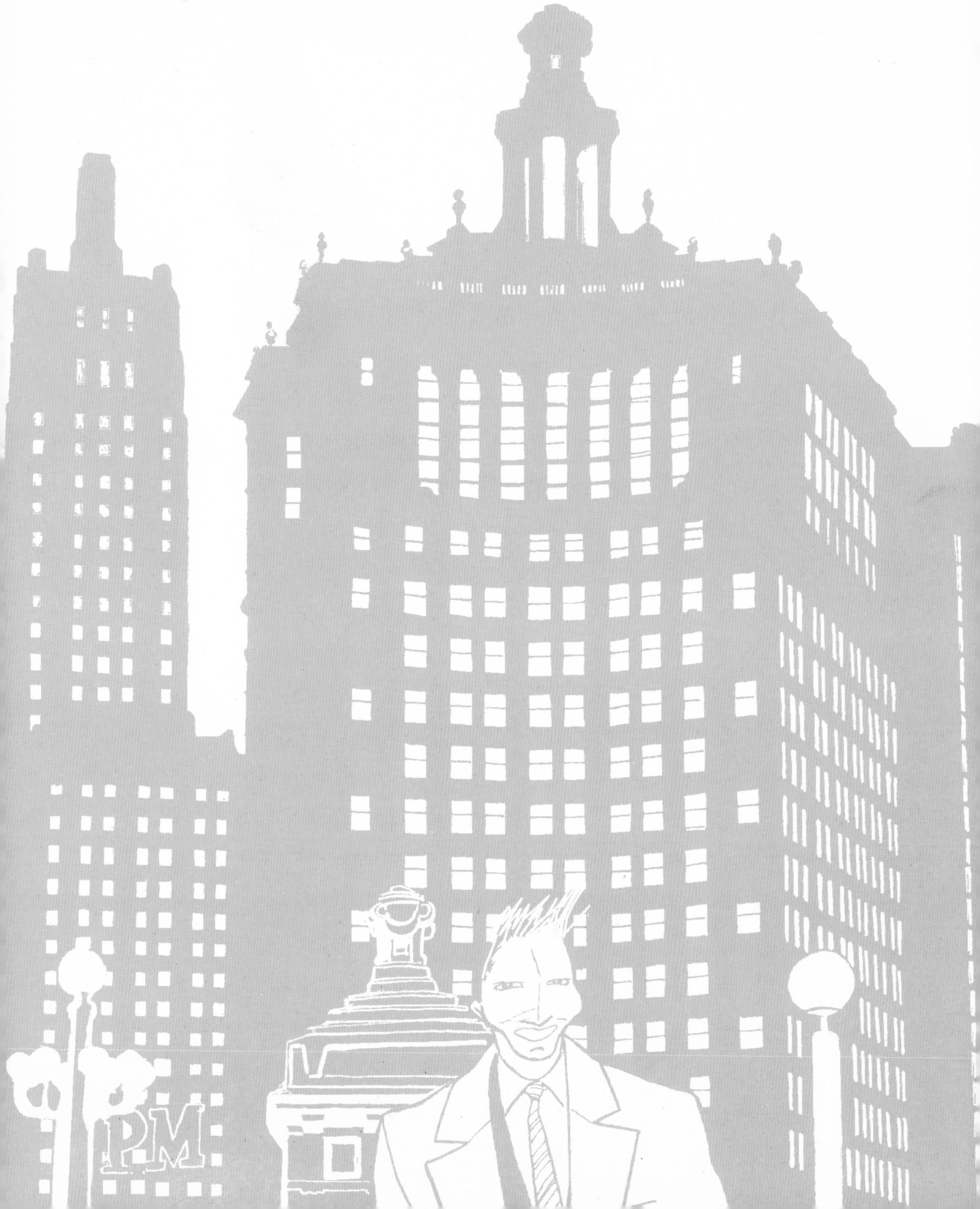
PM

ROAD TO AMERICA WAS ORIGINALLY SERIALIZED IN ENGLISH IN DRAWN & QUARTERLY VOLUME 2, #'S 4, 5, AND 6.

PUBLISHER: CHRIS OLIVEROS

FIRST EDITION: APRIL 2002
PRINTED BY COCONINO PRESS, BOLOGNA, ITALY
ISBN 1-896597-52-1
10 9 8 7 6 5 4 3 2 1

DRAWN & QUARTERLY
POST OFFICE BOX 48056
MONTREAL, QUEBEC
CANADA H2V 4S8

FREE CATALOGUE AVAILABLE UPON REQUEST.

WEBSITE: www.drawnandquarterly.com
E-MAIL: info@drawnandquarterly.com

DRAWN AND
D&Q
QUARTERLY

Road to America

BARU with JEAN-MARC THÉVENET

Road to America

BARU with JEAN-MARC THÉVENET

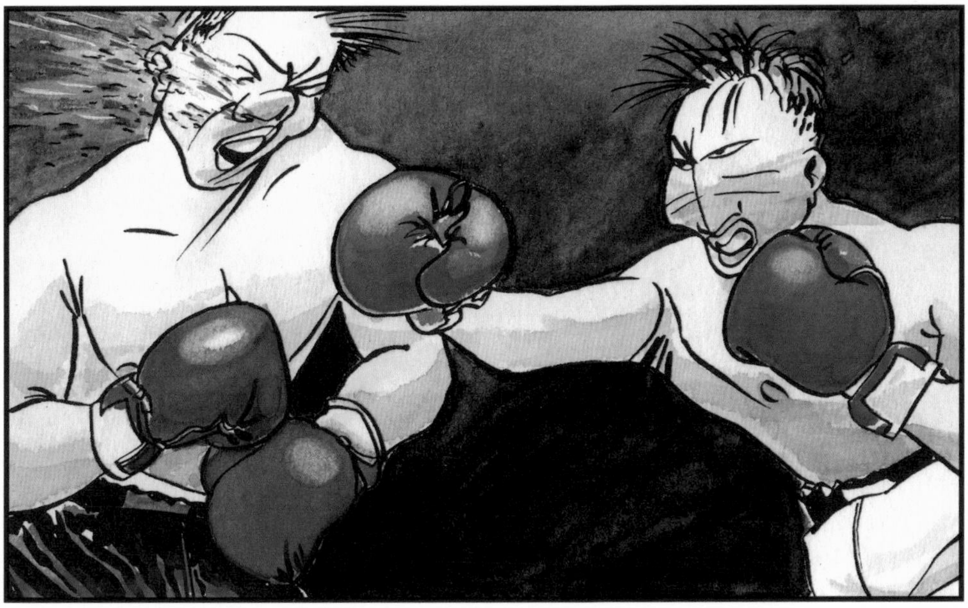

DRAWN AND QUARTERLY

STORY: BARU AND JEAN-MARC THÉVENET
ARTWORK: BARU
COLORS: DANIEL LEDRAN
TRANSLATION: HELGE DASCHER
LETTERING: DIRK REHM

THE ROAD TO AMERICA IS SET DURING ALGERIA'S LONG AND BLOODY STRUGGLE TO FREE ITSELF FROM FRENCH COLONIAL RULE. THE FLN (NATIONAL LIBERATION FRONT) SPEARHEADED THE FIGHT FOR INDEPENDENCE THROUGH A SERIES OF BOMBING CAMPAIGNS AND CLASHES WITH THE MILITARY AND, BY ITS END, THE CIVIL WAR HAD CLAIMED THE LIVES OF MORE THAN 150,000 ALGERIAN NATIONALISTS AND AT LEAST 10,000 FRENCH SOLDIERS. THE CLIMATE WAS SUCH THAT NO ALGERIAN COULD AFFORD NOT TO HAVE FIRM ALLEGIANCES WITH ONE SIDE, AND THOSE CAUGHT IN THE MIDDLE WERE DEALT WITH HARSHLY BY THE FLN. SAÏD BOUDIAF, THE STORY'S MAIN CHARACTER, COULDN'T HAVE PLACED HIMSELF FURTHER FROM THE MARGINS OF THIS POLITICAL CONTEXT. AMIDST THE CHAOS SURROUNDING HIM, HE HAS AS HIS ROLE MODEL MARCEL CERDAN, THE FAMED FRENCH BOXER KILLED IN A PLANE CRASH WHILE ON HIS WAY TO JOIN HIS LOVER EDITH PIAF IN AMERICA...

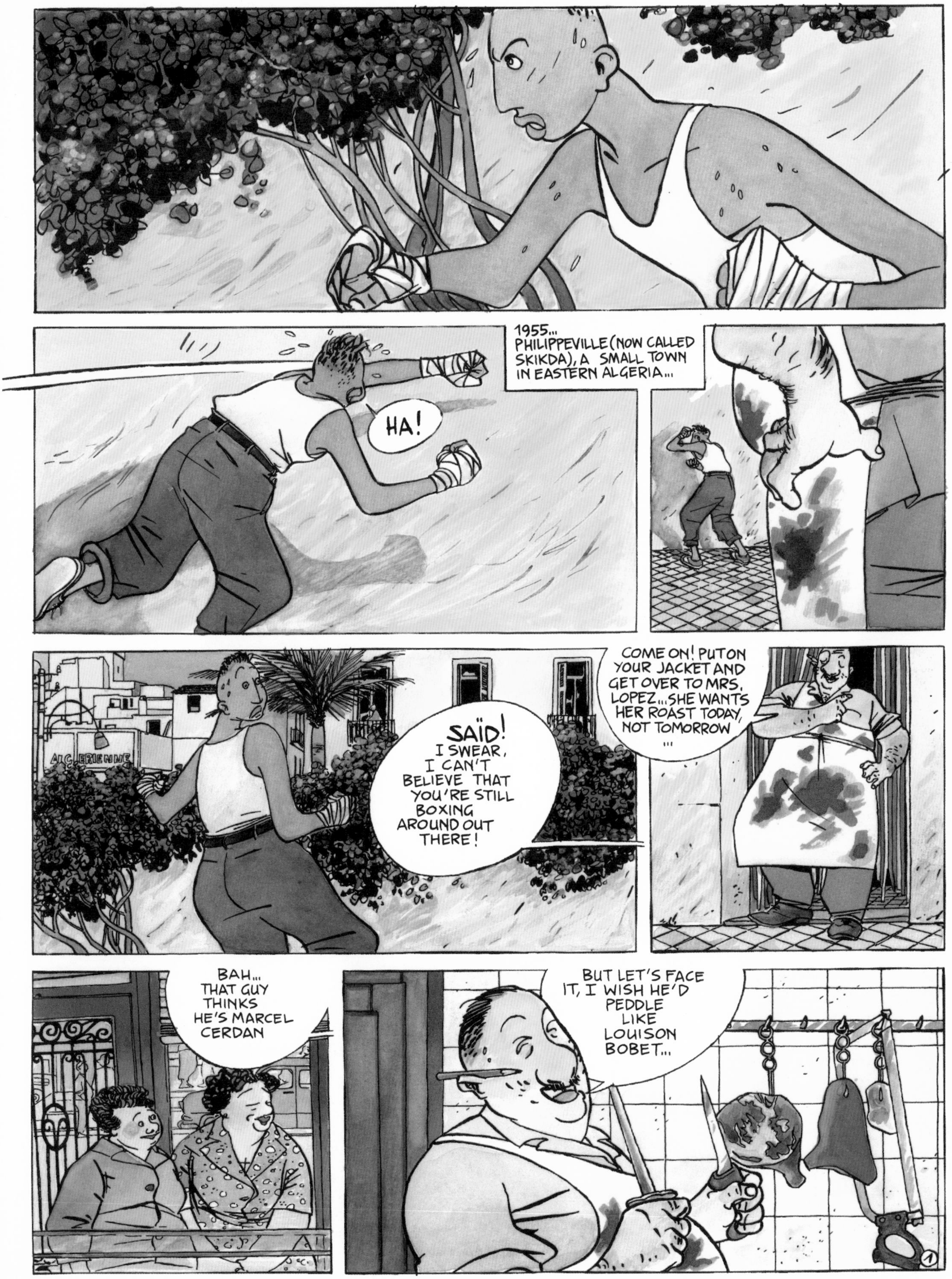

1955... PHILIPPEVILLE (NOW CALLED SKIKDA), A SMALL TOWN IN EASTERN ALGERIA...
HA!
COME ON! PUT ON YOUR JACKET AND GET OVER TO MRS. LOPEZ... SHE WANTS HER ROAST TODAY, NOT TOMORROW ...
SAÏD! I SWEAR, I CAN'T BELIEVE THAT YOU'RE STILL BOXING AROUND OUT THERE!
ALGERIENNE
BAH... THAT GUY THINKS HE'S MARCEL CERDAN
BUT LET'S FACE IT, I WISH HE'D PEDDLE LIKE LOUISON BOBET...
1

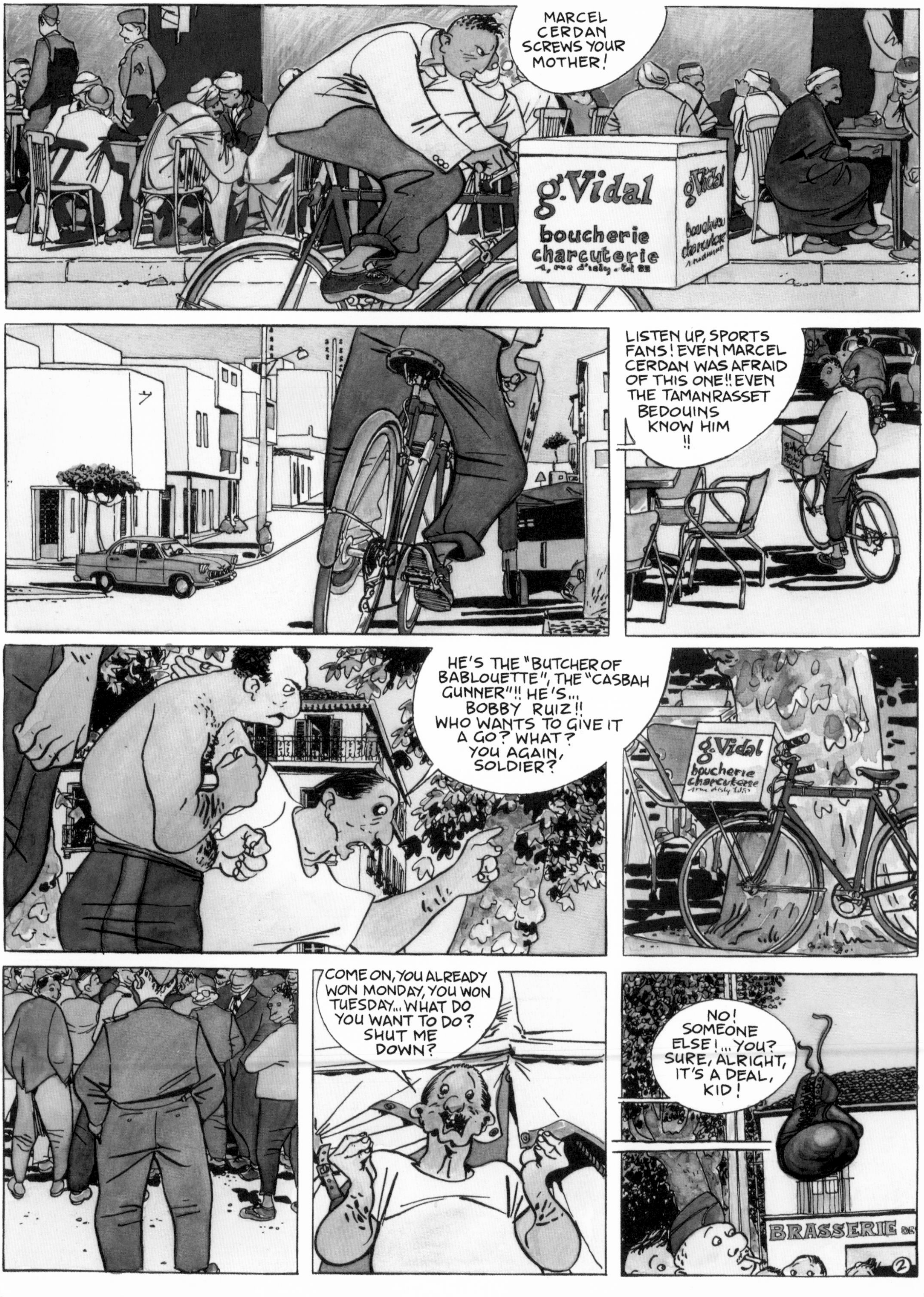
MARCEL CERDAN SCREWS YOUR MOTHER!
g.Vidal boucherie charcuterie
LISTEN UP, SPORTS FANS! EVEN MARCEL CERDAN WAS AFRAID OF THIS ONE!! EVEN THE TAMANRASSET BEDOUINS KNOW HIM !!
HE'S THE "BUTCHER OF BABLOUETTE", THE "CASBAH GUNNER"!! HE'S... BOBBY RUIZ!! WHO WANTS TO GIVE IT A GO? WHAT? YOU AGAIN, SOLDIER?
g.Vidal boucherie charcuterie
COME ON, YOU ALREADY WON MONDAY, YOU WON TUESDAY... WHAT DO YOU WANT TO DO? SHUT ME DOWN?
NO! SOMEONE ELSE!... YOU? SURE, ALRIGHT, IT'S A DEAL, KID!
BRASSERIE
2

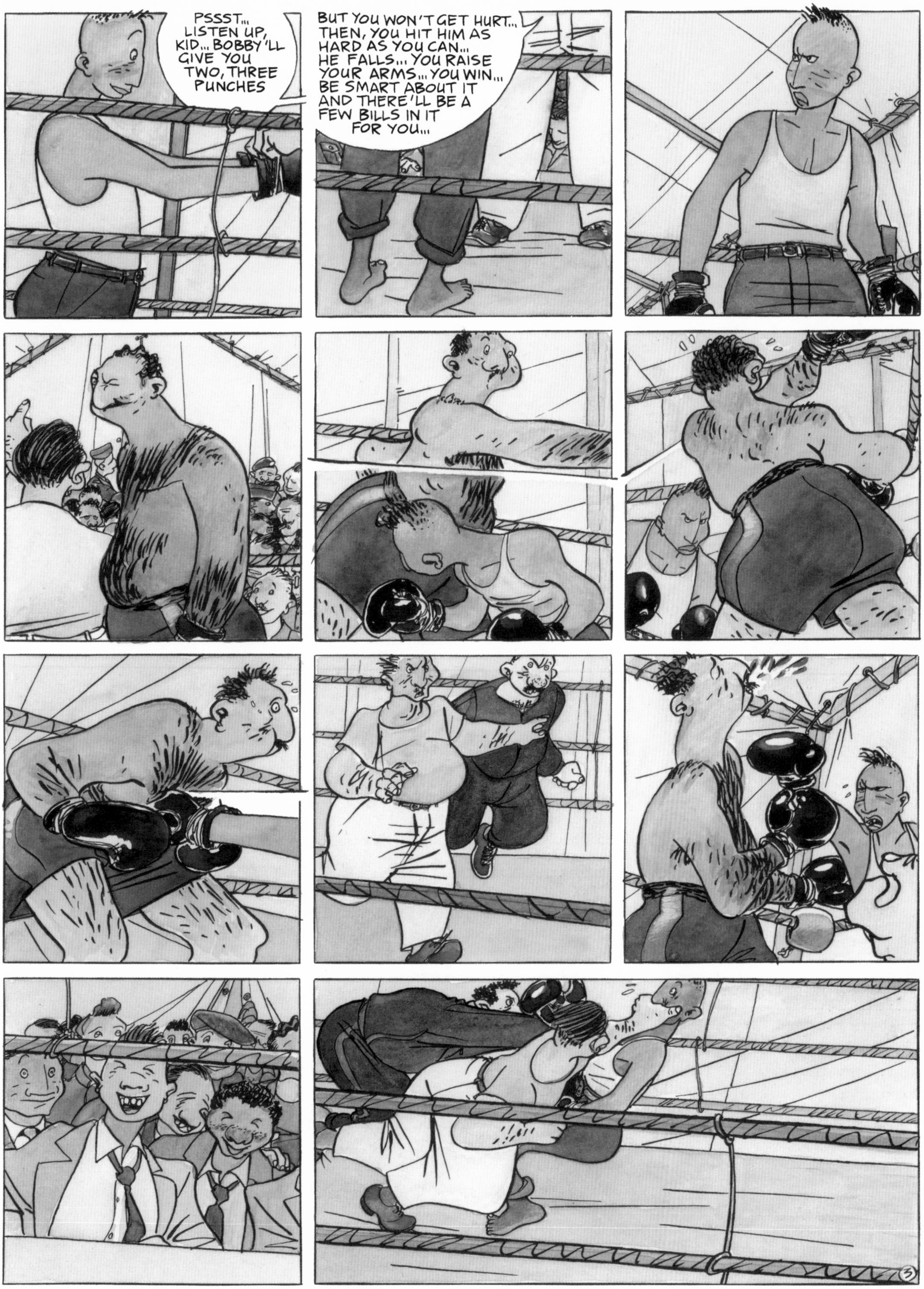
PSSST... LISTEN UP, KID... BOBBY'LL GIVE YOU TWO, THREE PUNCHES
BUT YOU WON'T GET HURT... THEN, YOU HIT HIM AS HARD AS YOU CAN... HE FALLS... YOU RAISE YOUR ARMS... YOU WIN... BE SMART ABOUT IT AND THERE'LL BE A FEW BILLS IN IT FOR YOU...

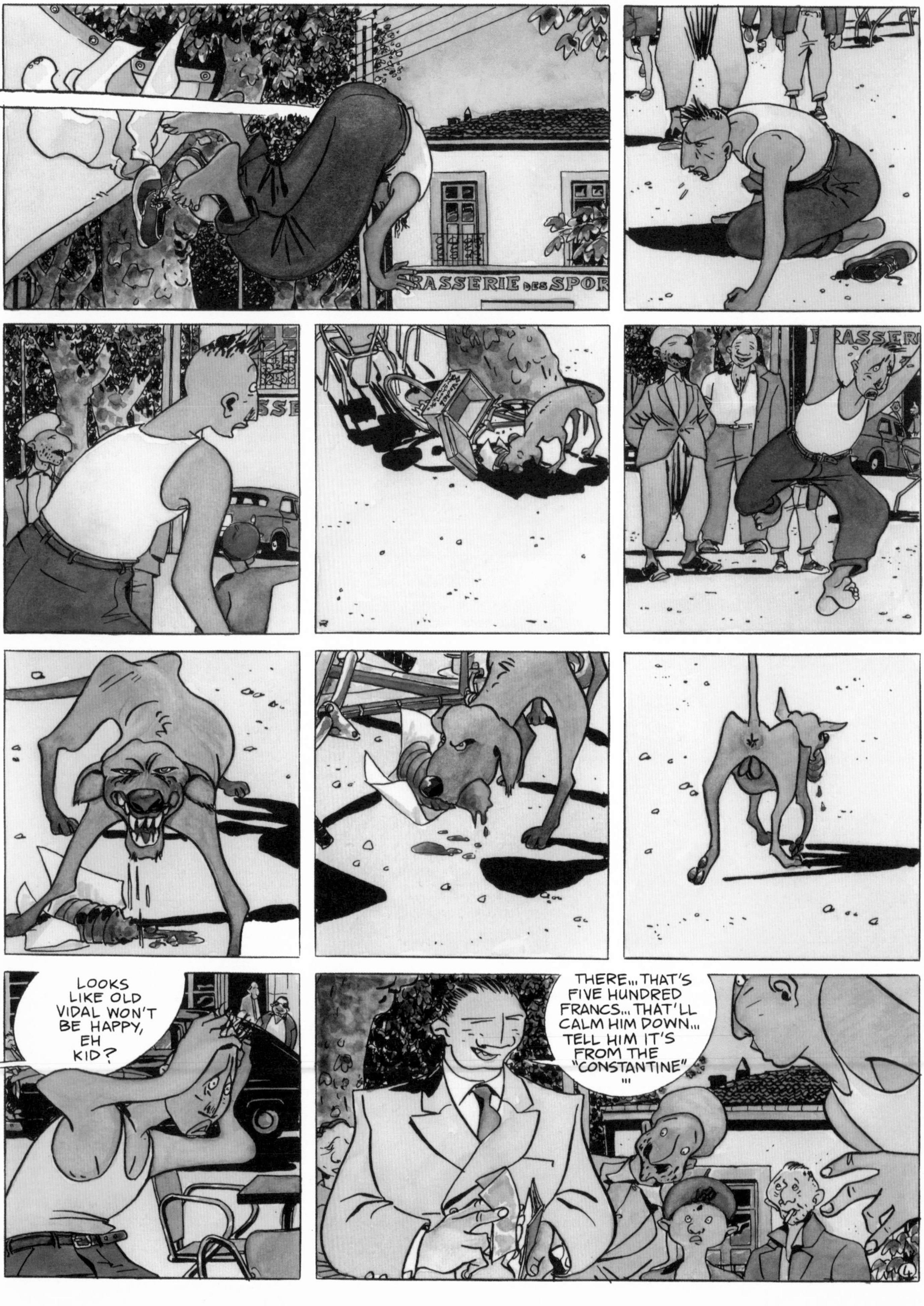

RASSERIE DES SPOR
LOOKS LIKE OLD VIDAL WON'T BE HAPPY, EH KID?
THERE... THAT'S FIVE HUNDRED FRANCS... THAT'LL CALM HIM DOWN... TELL HIM IT'S FROM THE "CONSTANTINE"...

TELL ME... HOW WOULD YOU LIKE TO DO SOME REAL BOXING?...
BOXING!! M...ME?!!
PEPSI-COL

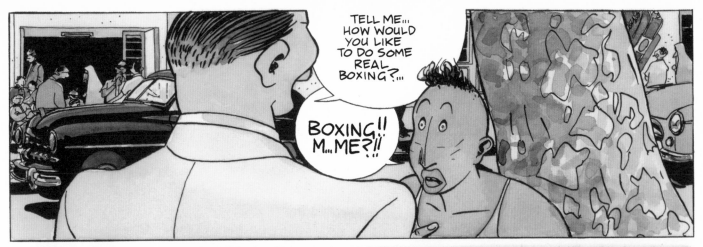

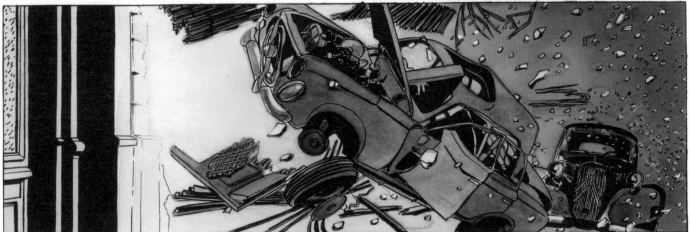

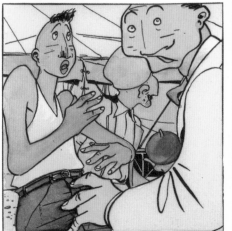

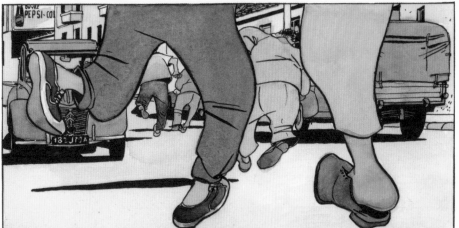

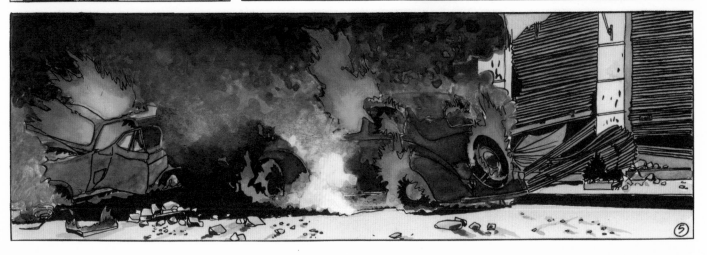

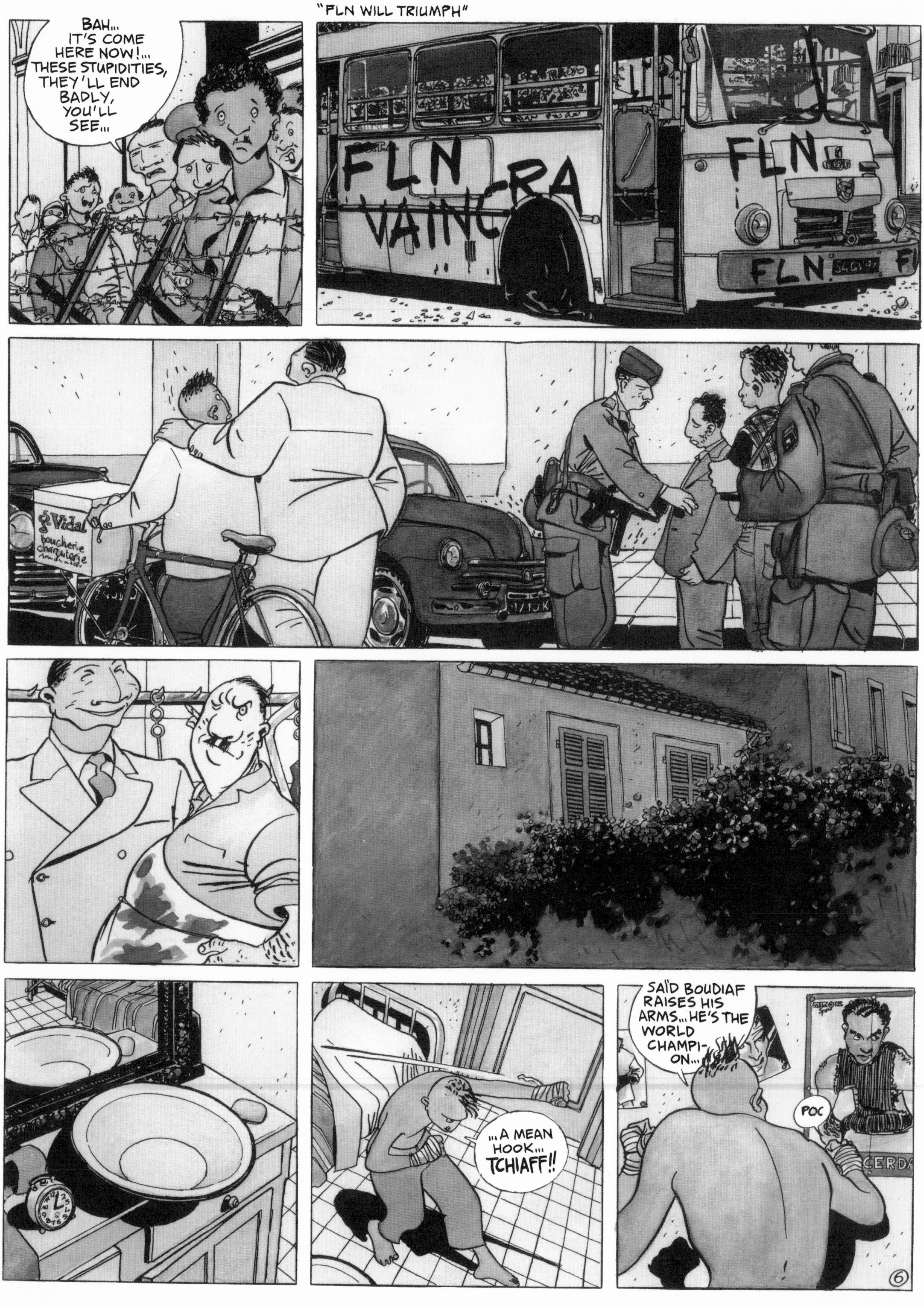
BAH... IT'S COME HERE NOW!... THESE STUPIDITIES, THEY'LL END BADLY, YOU'LL SEE...
"FLN WILL TRIUMPH"
FLN VAINCRA
FLN
FLN
Vidal boucherie charcuterie
SAÏD BOUDIAF RAISES HIS ARMS... HE'S THE WORLD CHAMPI-ON...
...A MEAN HOOK... TCHIAFF!!
POC
CERDA
6

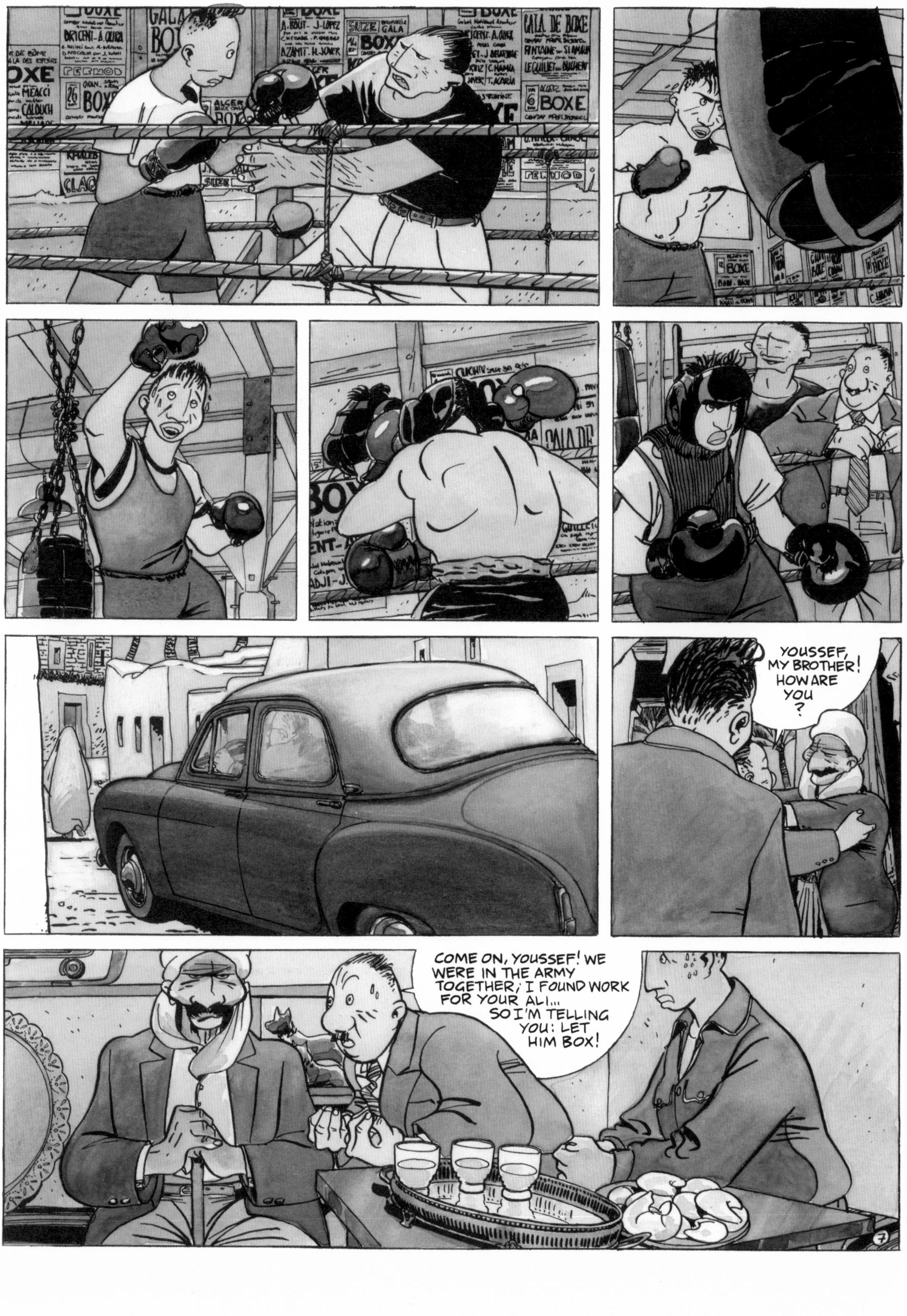
YOUSSEF, MY BROTHER! HOW ARE YOU ?
COME ON, YOUSSEF! WE WERE IN THE ARMY TOGETHER; I FOUND WORK FOR YOUR ALI... SO I'M TELLING YOU: LET HIM BOX!

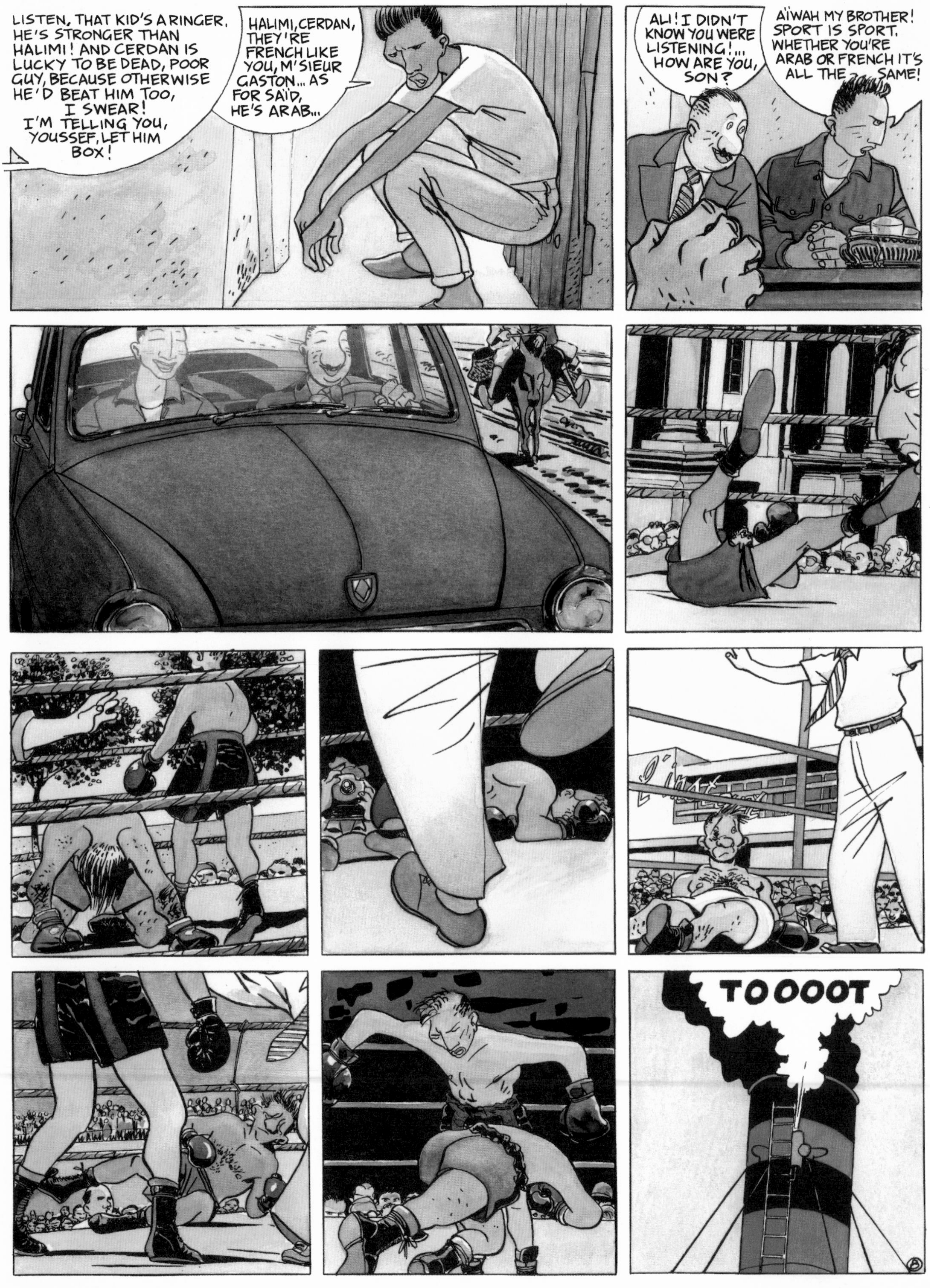
LISTEN, THAT KID'S A RINGER. HE'S STRONGER THAN HALIMI! AND CERDAN IS LUCKY TO BE DEAD, POOR GUY, BECAUSE OTHERWISE HE'D BEAT HIM TOO, I SWEAR! I'M TELLING YOU, YOUSSEF, LET HIM BOX!
HALIMI, CERDAN, THEY'RE FRENCH LIKE YOU, M'SIEUR GASTON... AS FOR SAÏD, HE'S ARAB...
ALI! I DIDN'T KNOW YOU WERE LISTENING!... HOW ARE YOU, SON?
AÏWAH MY BROTHER! SPORT IS SPORT. WHETHER YOU'RE ARAB OR FRENCH IT'S ALL THE SAME!
TOOOOT

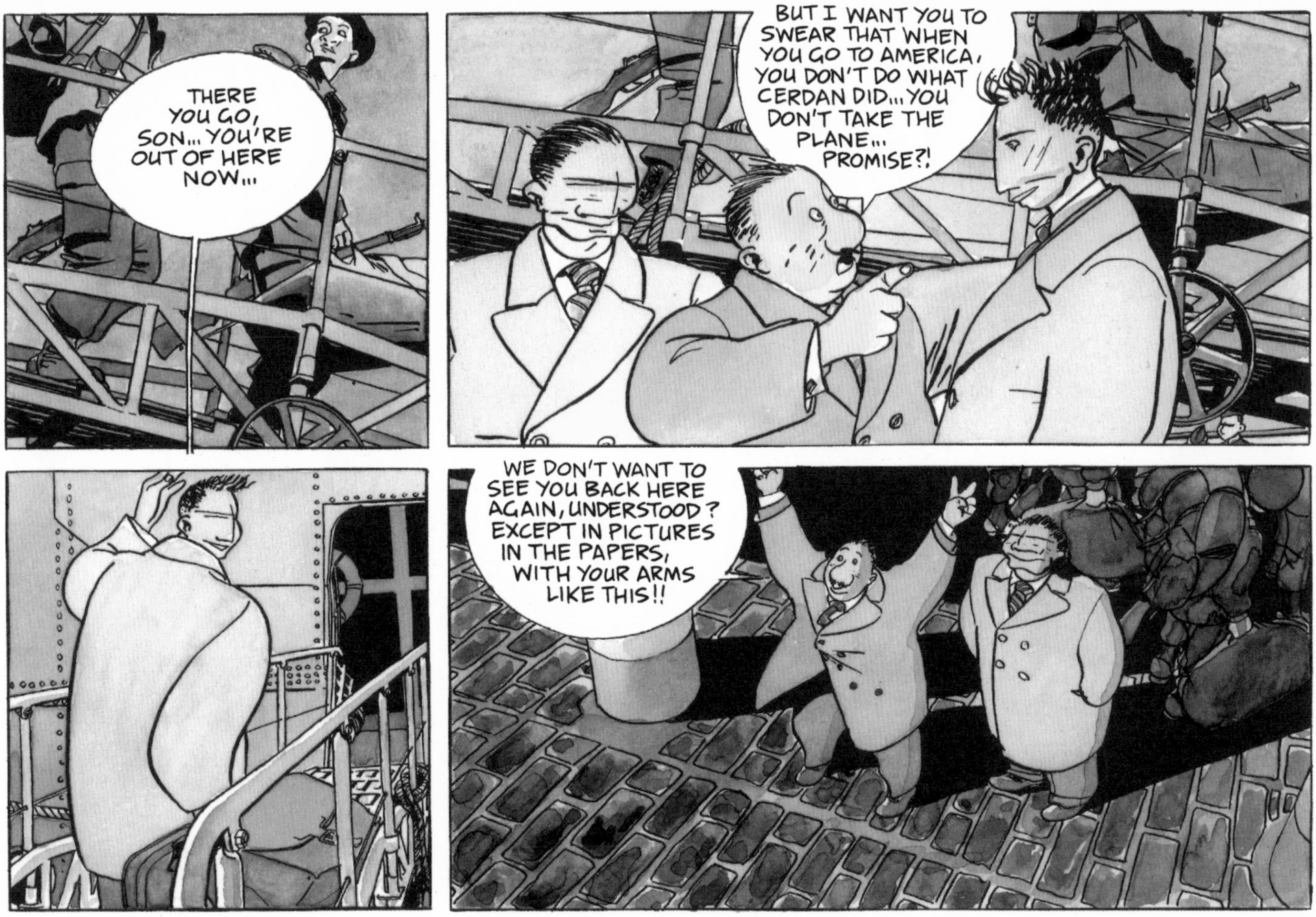
THERE YOU GO, SON... YOU'RE OUT OF HERE NOW...
BUT I WANT YOU TO SWEAR THAT WHEN YOU GO TO AMERICA, YOU DON'T DO WHAT CERDAN DID... YOU DON'T TAKE THE PLANE... PROMISE?!
WE DON'T WANT TO SEE YOU BACK HERE AGAIN, UNDERSTOOD? EXCEPT IN PICTURES IN THE PAPERS, WITH YOUR ARMS LIKE THIS!!

Saïd, my dear brother.
As you can see I still manage to write proper French. I am sending you this letter to tell you that I'm also leaving. I'm enlisting in the French army but I won't stay. I'll wait till I've got my rifle and then I'll join the resistance. I'm sorry if it hurts you. I wish you good luck and may god be with you. Your brother thinks of you.

Ali

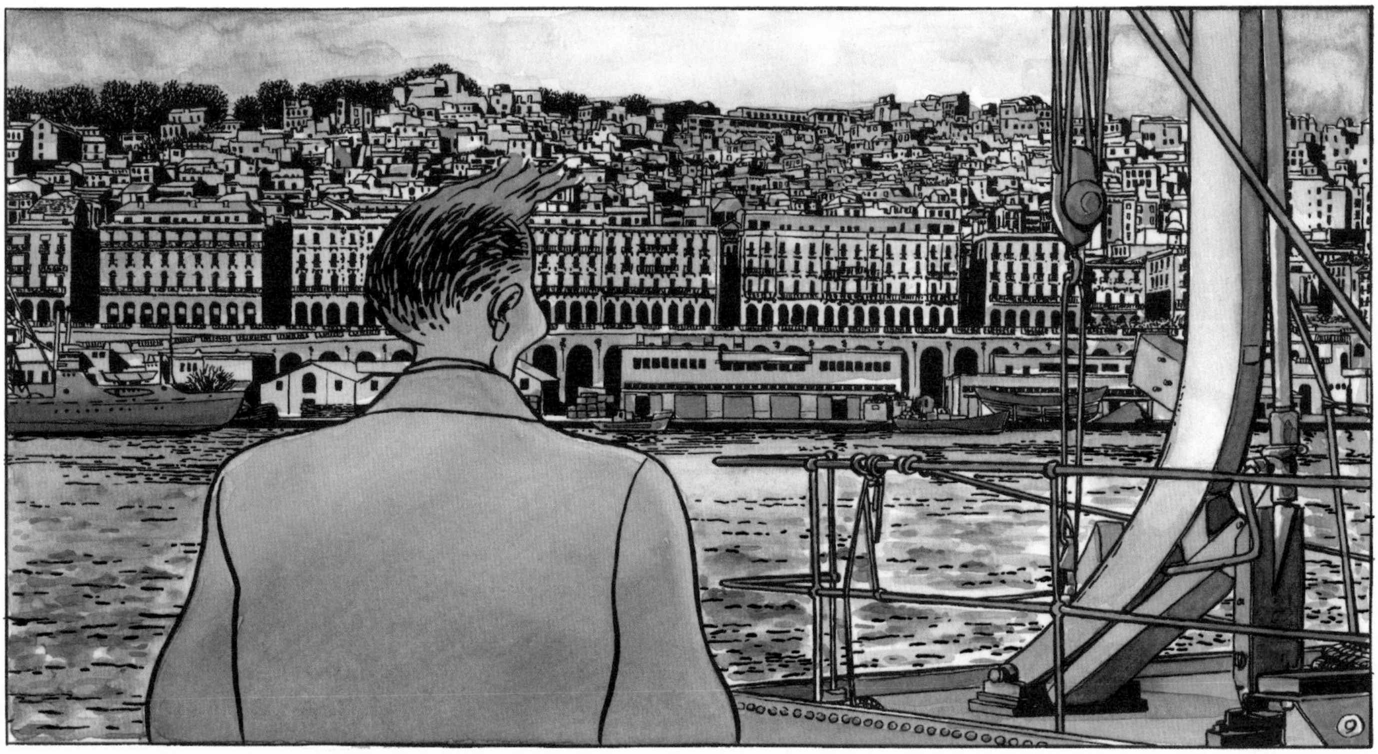

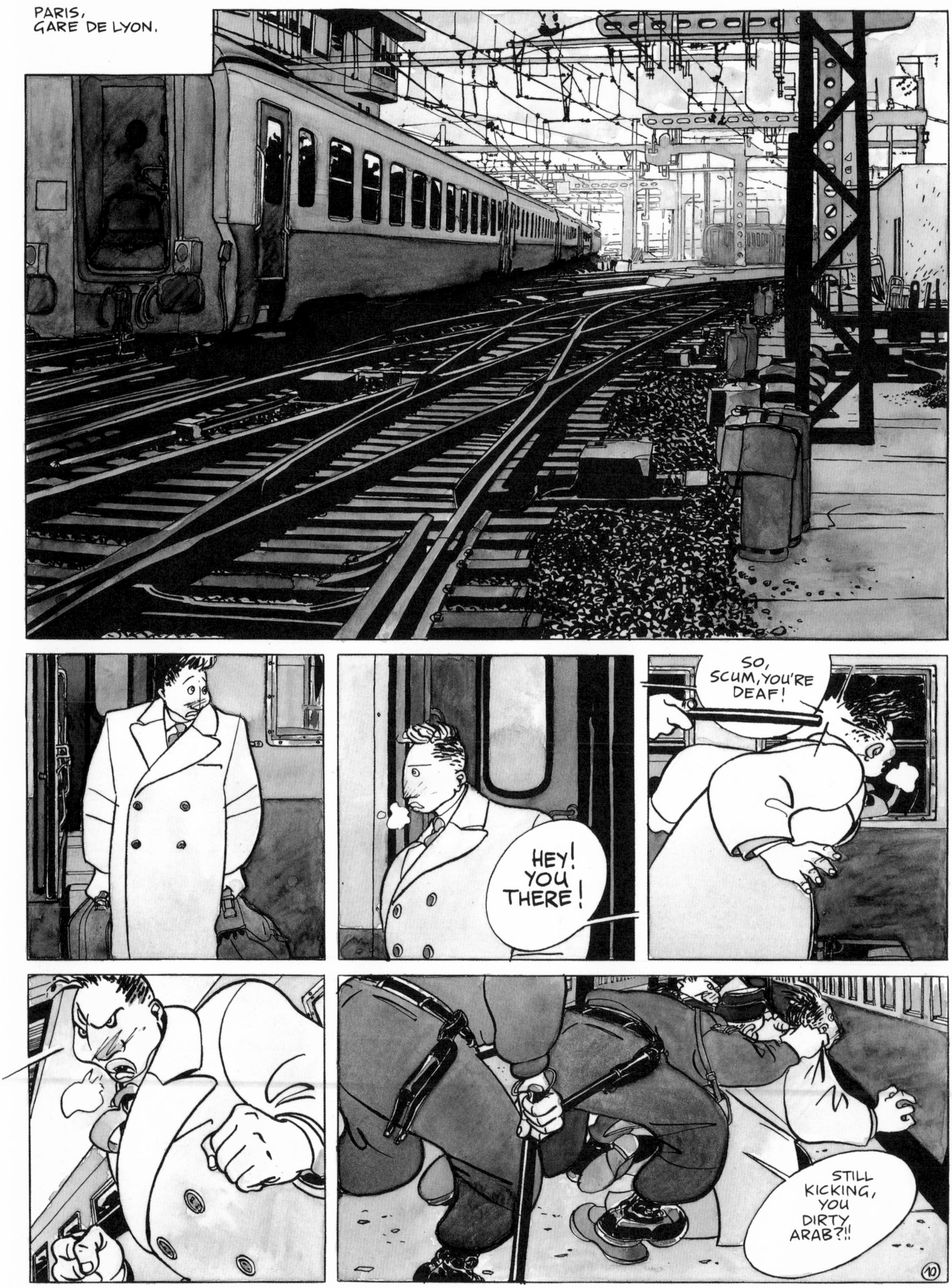
PARIS,
GARE DE LYON.
HEY! YOU THERE!
SO, SCUM, YOU'RE DEAF!
STILL KICKING, YOU DIRTY ARAB?!!

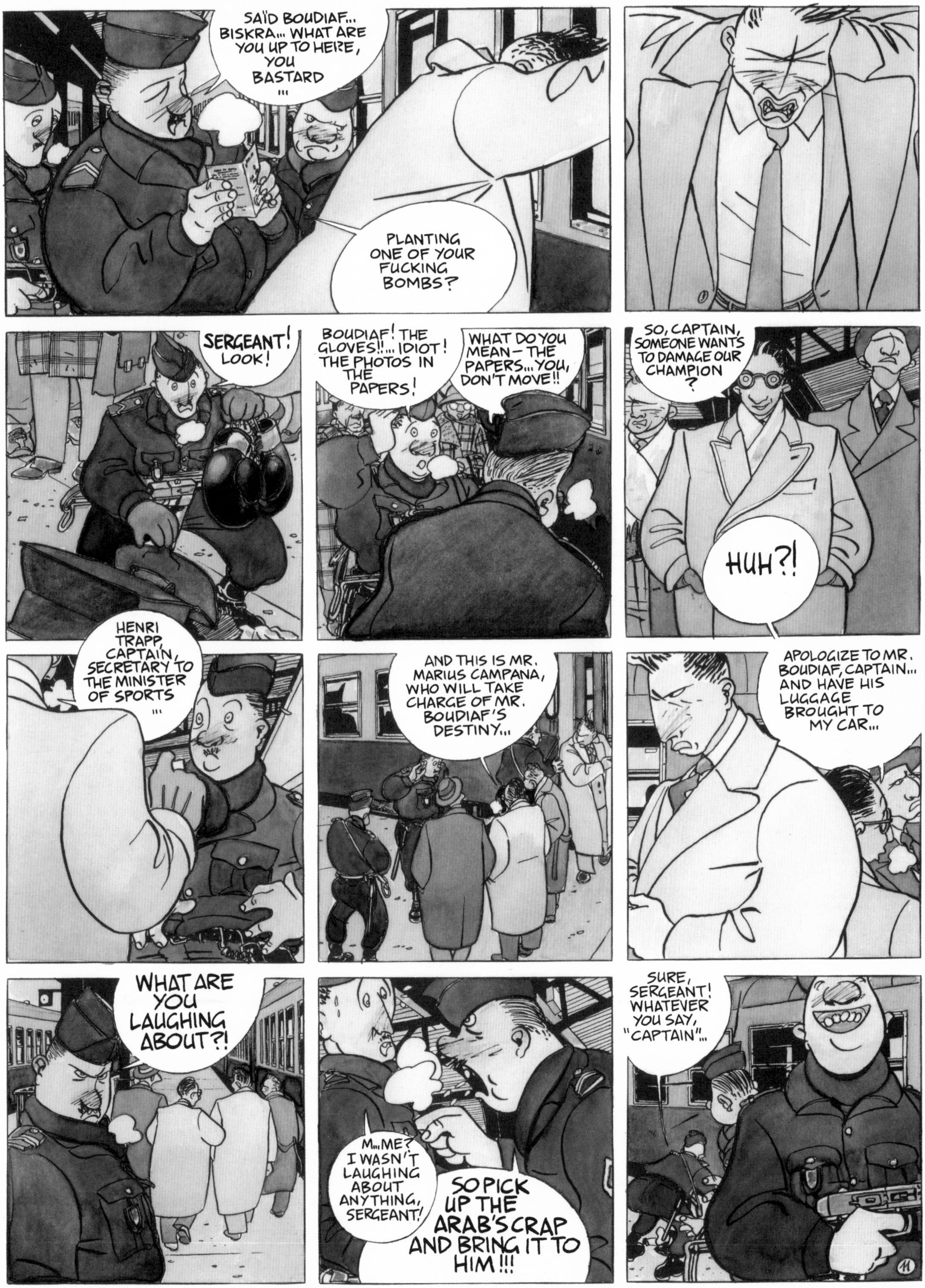

SAÏD BOUDIAF... BISKRA... WHAT ARE YOU UP TO HERE, YOU BASTARD ...
PLANTING ONE OF YOUR FUCKING BOMBS?
SERGEANT! LOOK!
BOUDIAF! THE GLOVES!!... IDIOT! THE PHOTOS IN THE PAPERS!
WHAT DO YOU MEAN – THE PAPERS... YOU, DON'T MOVE!!
SO, CAPTAIN, SOMEONE WANTS TO DAMAGE OUR CHAMPION ?
HUH?!
HENRI TRAPP, CAPTAIN, SECRETARY TO THE MINISTER OF SPORTS ...
AND THIS IS MR. MARIUS CAMPANA, WHO WILL TAKE CHARGE OF MR. BOUDIAF'S DESTINY...
APOLOGIZE TO MR. BOUDIAF, CAPTAIN... AND HAVE HIS LUGGAGE BROUGHT TO MY CAR...
WHAT ARE YOU LAUGHING ABOUT?!
M...ME? I WASN'T LAUGHING ABOUT ANYTHING, SERGEANT!
SO PICK UP THE ARAB'S CRAP AND BRING IT TO HIM!!!
SURE, SERGEANT! WHATEVER YOU SAY, "CAPTAIN"...
11

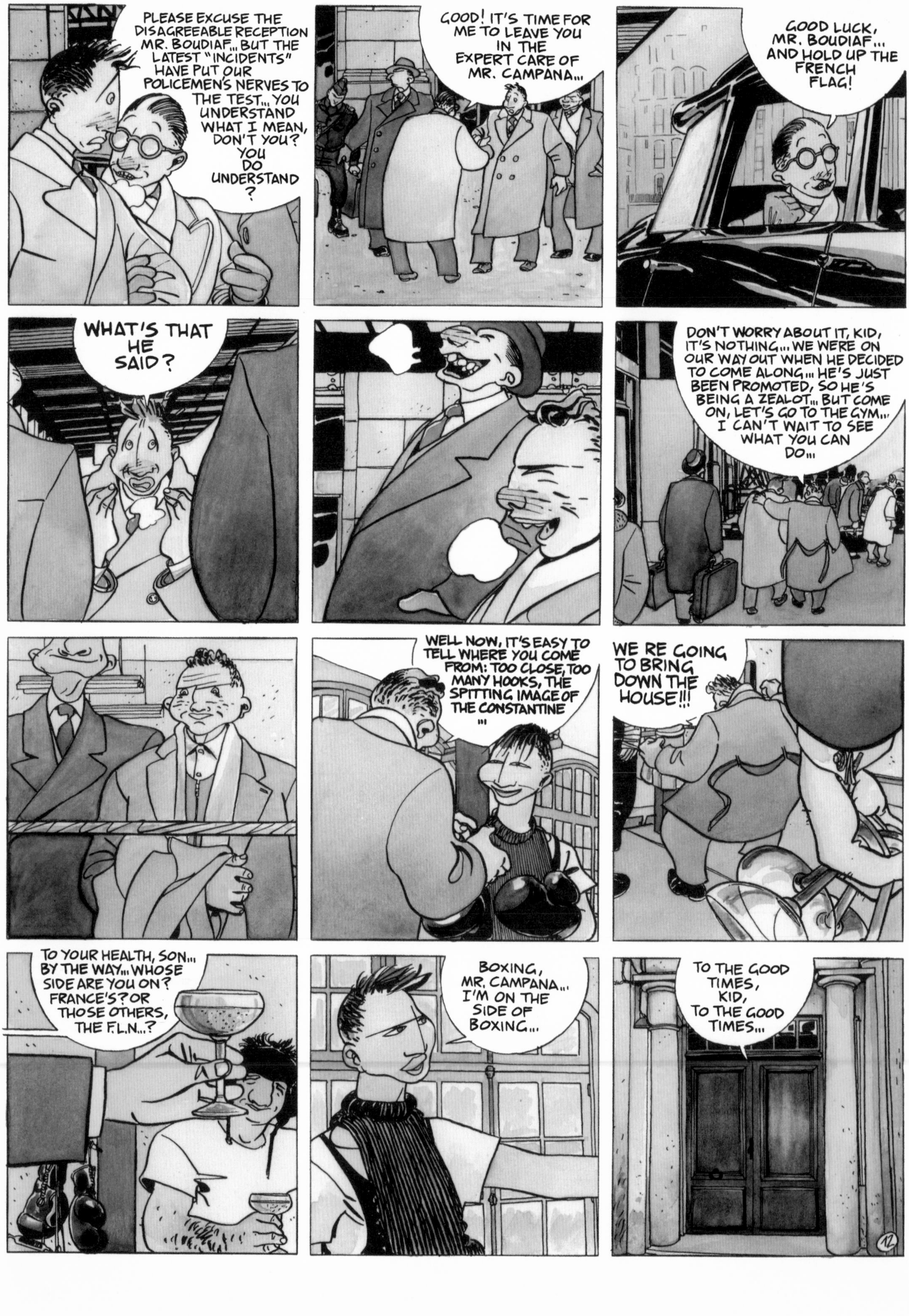
PLEASE EXCUSE THE DISAGREEABLE RECEPTION MR. BOUDIAF... BUT THE LATEST "INCIDENTS" HAVE PUT OUR POLICEMEN'S NERVES TO THE TEST... YOU UNDERSTAND WHAT I MEAN, DON'T YOU? YOU DO UNDERSTAND ?
GOOD! IT'S TIME FOR ME TO LEAVE YOU IN THE EXPERT CARE OF MR. CAMPANA...
GOOD LUCK, MR. BOUDIAF... AND HOLD UP THE FRENCH FLAG!
WHAT'S THAT HE SAID?
DON'T WORRY ABOUT IT, KID, IT'S NOTHING... WE WERE ON OUR WAY OUT WHEN HE DECIDED TO COME ALONG... HE'S JUST BEEN PROMOTED, SO HE'S BEING A ZEALOT... BUT COME ON, LET'S GO TO THE GYM... I CAN'T WAIT TO SEE WHAT YOU CAN DO...
WELL NOW, IT'S EASY TO TELL WHERE YOU COME FROM: TOO CLOSE, TOO MANY HOOKS, THE SPITTING IMAGE OF THE CONSTANTINE ...
WE RE GOING TO BRING DOWN THE HOUSE!!!
TO YOUR HEALTH, SON... BY THE WAY... WHOSE SIDE ARE YOU ON? FRANCE'S? OR THOSE OTHERS, THE F.L.N...?
BOXING, MR. CAMPANA... I'M ON THE SIDE OF BOXING...
TO THE GOOD TIMES, KID, TO THE GOOD TIMES...
12

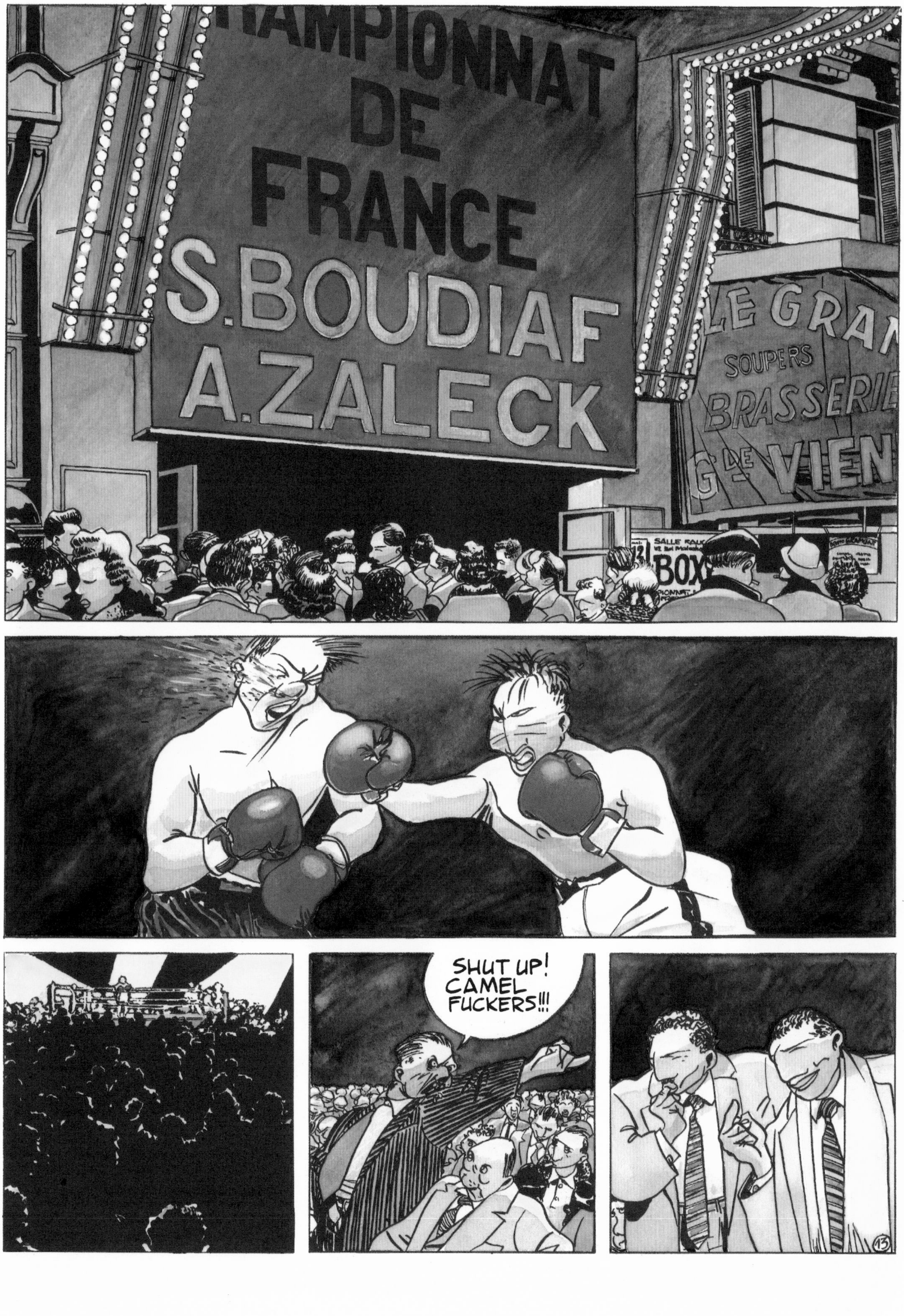
HAMPIONNAT
DE
FRANCE
S.BOUDIAF
A.ZALECK
LE GRAN
SOUPERS
BRASSERIE
Gde VIEN
BOX
SHUT UP! CAMEL FUCKERS!!!

Saïd Boudiaf- André Zaleck

PLACE: RAUGRAFF HALL - PARIS
DATE: DECEMBER 12, 1958
ATTENDANCE: 4,152

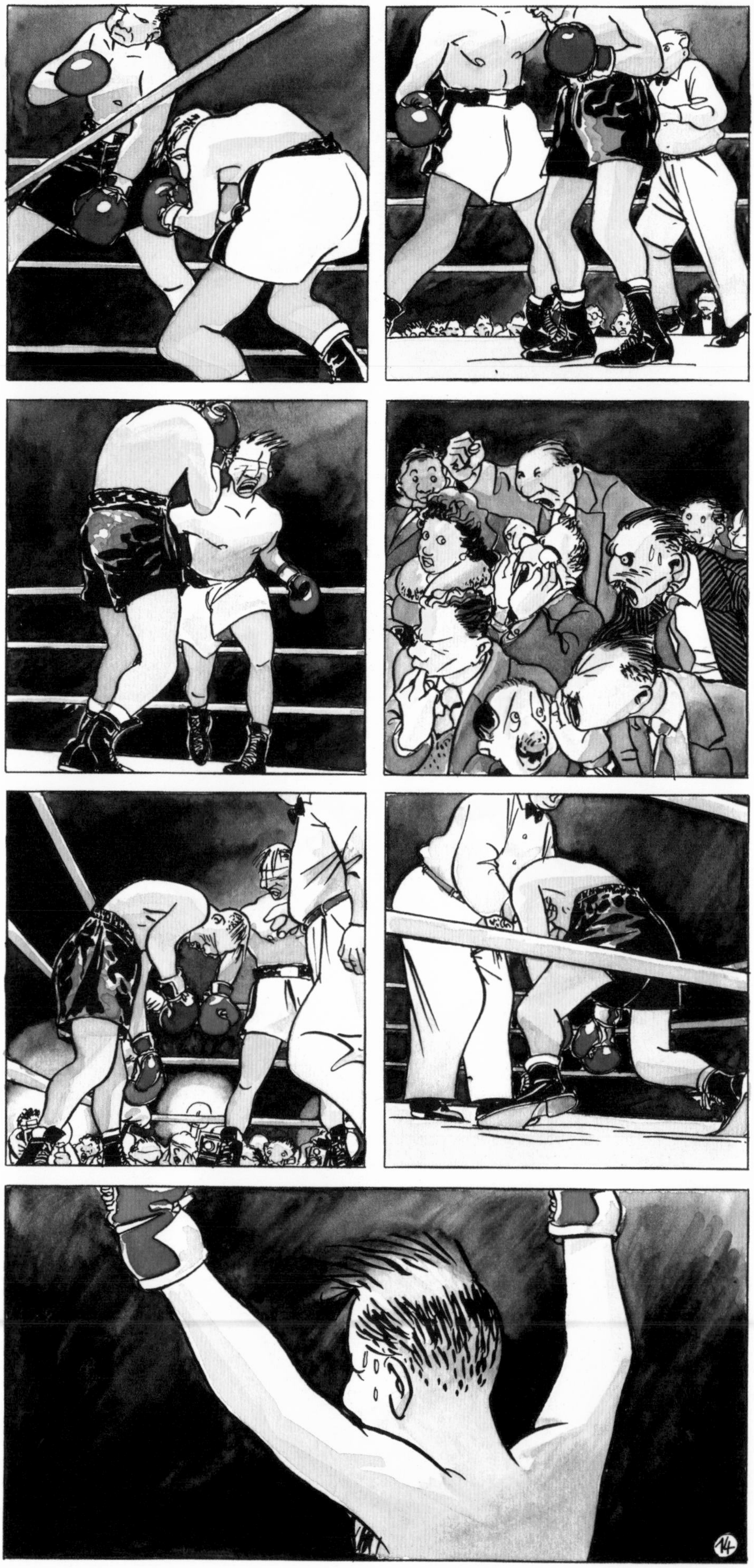

1st round

ZALECK, AS USUAL, ATTACKS IMMEDIATELY. BUT HIS PUNCHES ONLY GLANCE THE ARMS OF BOUDIAF WHO COUNTERS. ZALECK ATTACKS AGAIN, UPPERCUT TO THE STOMACH, LEFT AND RIGHT HOOKS, LEFT TO THE BODY. BOUDIAF STEPS BACK AND LETS THE STORM PASS. ADVANTAGE ZALECK.

2nd round

ZALECK RUSHES TO ATTACK BUT IS STOPPED CLEAN BY A RIGHT-HANDER. BOUDIAF DOESN'T LET UP. HE HAS CHANGED HIS TACTIC: MOVE IN TO KEEP THE OPPONENT FROM MOVING IN. AT LAST HE GETS A CHANCE TO DISPLAY HIS INCOMPARABLE BOXING. HE HITS AND HITS AGAIN. HE ACCELERATES. ZALECK CLINCHES AND PAYS FOR IT BY TAKING A VICIOUS RIGHT.
ADVANTAGE BOUDIAF.

3rd round

BOUDIAF NEEDS A BREAK. BOTH MEN BOX CLOSE UP - EVERY PUNCH HURTS - THE FIGHT IS HARD TO FOLLOW - BOUDIAF SLIPS, HIS KNEE TOUCHES THE GROUND BUT HE BOUNCES BACK UP TO RESUME THE FIGHT - BOUDIAF SENDS A RIGHT HOOK TO THE CHIN - ZALECK IS HIT! HE PULLS HIMSELF UP AND ATTACKS IMMEDIATELY, AGGRESSIVE AND FURIOUS.
EQUAL.

4th round

ZALECK HAS REGAINED HIS CONFIDENCE. A RIGHT TOUCHES BOUDIAF ON THE JAW - HE COUNTERS WITH A MEAN LEFT HOOK - AND IT'S AN AVALANCHE - SAÏD BOUDIAF IS WILD. SERIES OF HOOKS WITH BOTH HANDS. ZALECK HOLDS ON. UPPERCUT AND A PERFECT LEFT HOOK - ZALECK IS STILL STANDING - DEVASTATING LEFT HOOK - THE AUDIENCE JEERS - SUDDENLY ZALECK'S HEAD SINKS SLOWLY ONTO BOUDIAF'S GLOVES... BOUDIAF MOVES BACK A STEP AND ZALECK FALLS, SLOW MOTION, THE REFEREE FOLLOWING HIM DOWN.
SAÏD BOUDIAF RAISES HIS ARMS. HE IS THE CHAMPION OF FRANCE. HE IS TWENTY-TWO YEARS OLD.

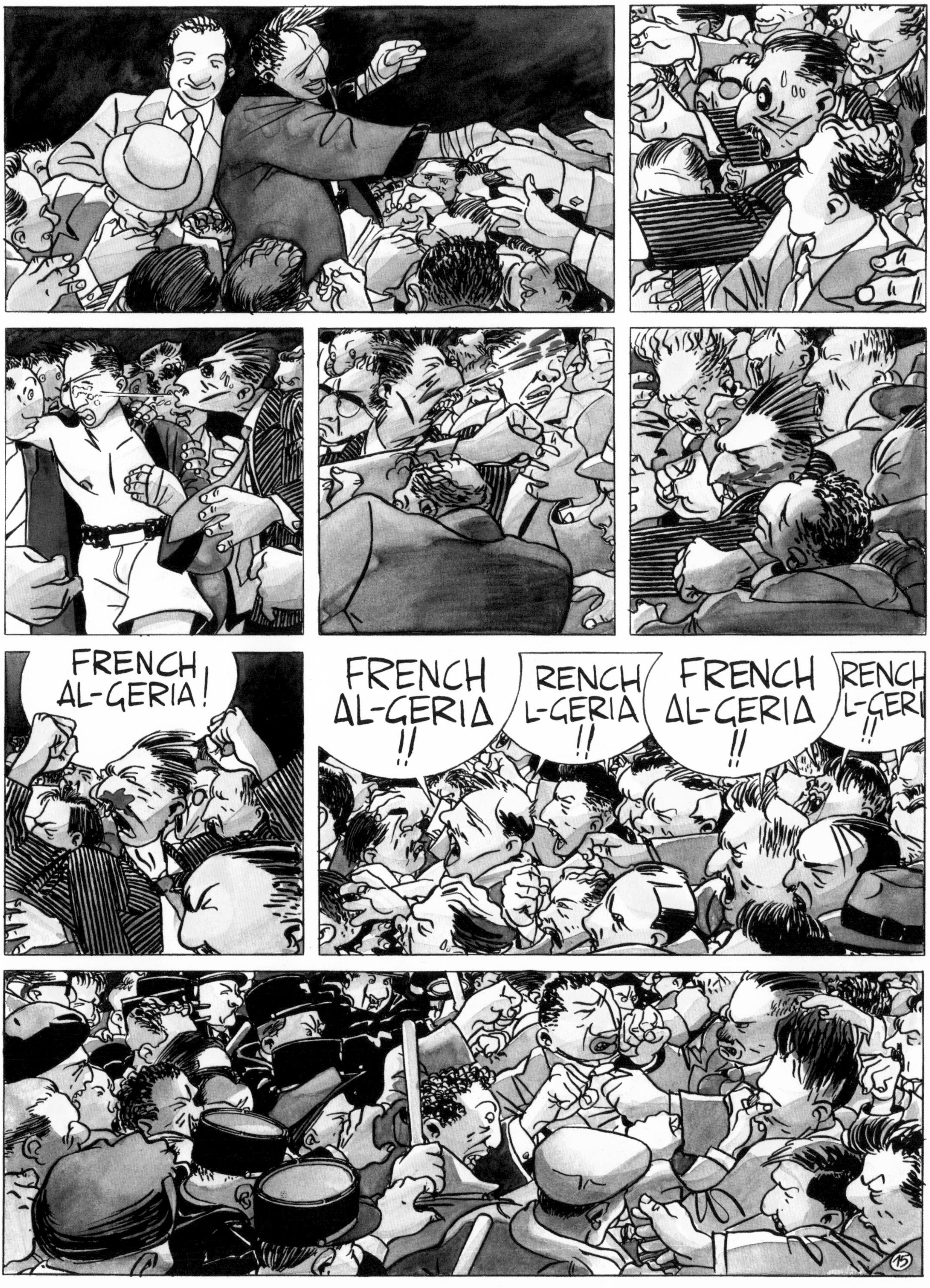
FRENCH AL-GERIA!
FRENCH AL-GERIA !!
RENCH L-GERIA !!
FRENCH AL-GERIA !!
RENCH L-GERI !!

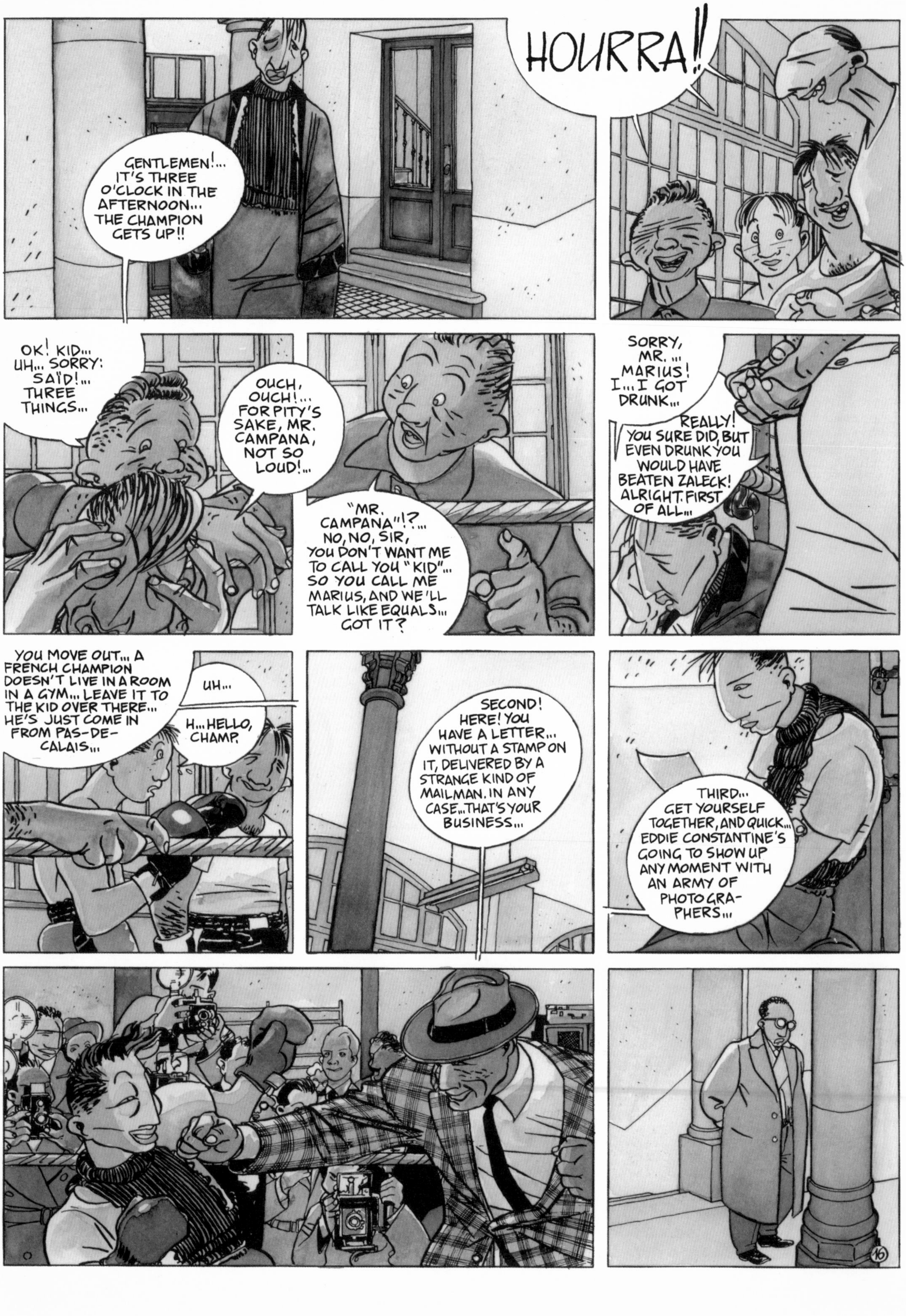
GENTLEMEN!... IT'S THREE O'CLOCK IN THE AFTERNOON... THE CHAMPION GETS UP!!
HOURRA!!
OK! KID... UH... SORRY: SAÏD!... THREE THINGS...
OUCH, OUCH!... FOR PITY'S SAKE, MR. CAMPANA, NOT SO LOUD!...
"MR. CAMPANA"!?... NO, NO, SIR, YOU DON'T WANT ME TO CALL YOU "KID"... SO YOU CALL ME MARIUS, AND WE'LL TALK LIKE EQUALS... GOT IT?
SORRY, MR. ... MARIUS! I... I GOT DRUNK...
REALLY! YOU SURE DID, BUT EVEN DRUNK YOU WOULD HAVE BEATEN ZALECK! ALRIGHT. FIRST OF ALL...
YOU MOVE OUT... A FRENCH CHAMPION DOESN'T LIVE IN A ROOM IN A GYM... LEAVE IT TO THE KID OVER THERE... HE'S JUST COME IN FROM PAS-DE-CALAIS...
UH...
H... HELLO, CHAMP.
SECOND! HERE! YOU HAVE A LETTER... WITHOUT A STAMP ON IT, DELIVERED BY A STRANGE KIND OF MAILMAN. IN ANY CASE... THAT'S YOUR BUSINESS...
THIRD... GET YOURSELF TOGETHER, AND QUICK... EDDIE CONSTANTINE'S GOING TO SHOW UP ANY MOMENT WITH AN ARMY OF PHOTOGRAPHERS...
16

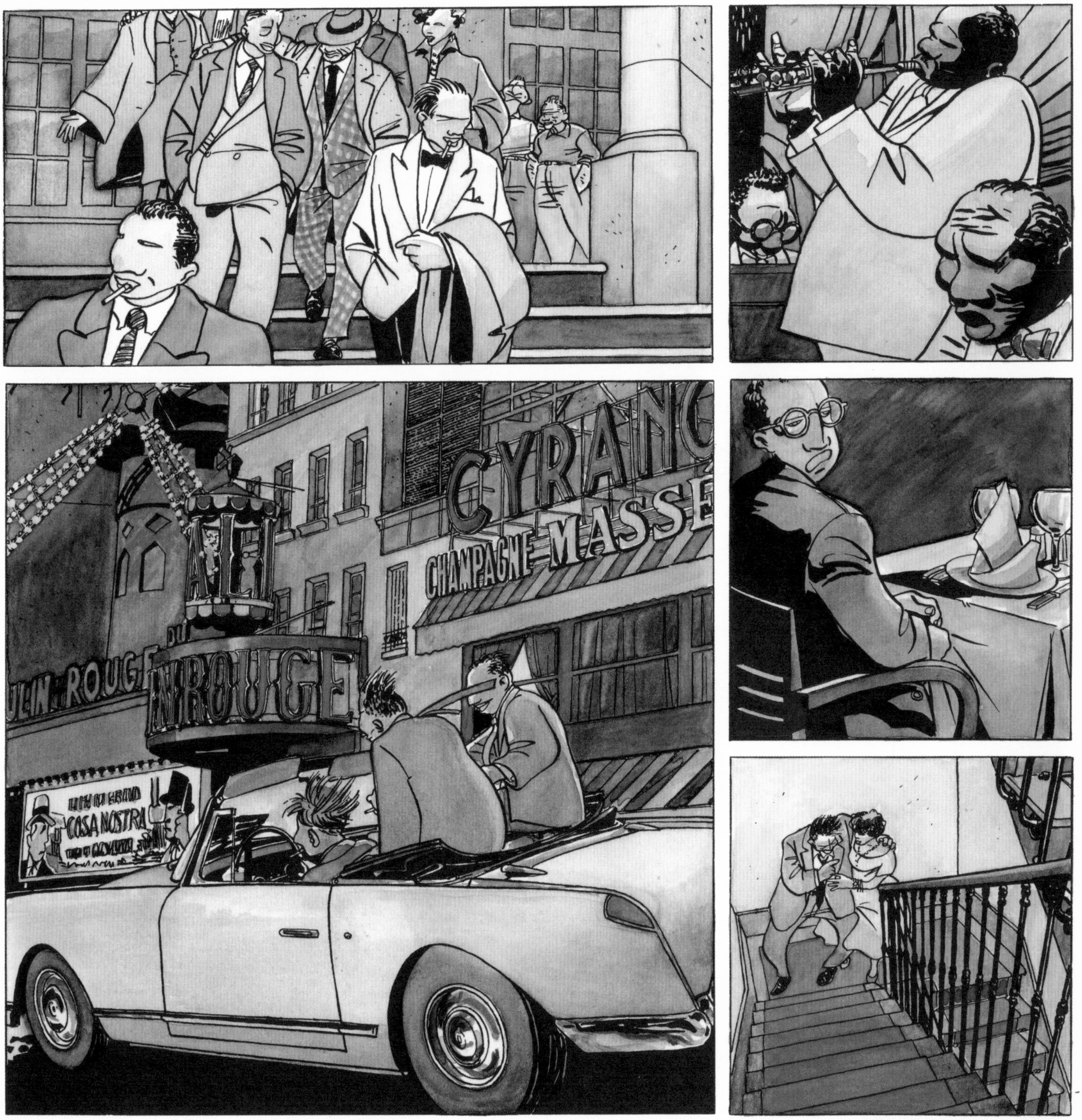
CYRANO
CHAMPAGNE MASSE
ALI
MOULIN ROUGE
DU
MOULIN ROUGE
COSA NOSTRA

Ali, my dear brother,
I am the symbol of nothing at all! I'm not fighting for the Algerian people. I'm fighting for myself, for you, for our family and for my friends. And they're French! And the money that I'm earning, I'm earning for me, for you, and for them. Not for the F.L.N., not to kill people. I'm telling you, Ali, I won't pay this tax. Mekloufi, Maouche and Chabri and all the others can do what they want, but I won't do it.
And why can't I write to you at home anymore? Why all these flunky spies with the kid from the Pigalle?
You are afraid that I'll forget that I'm Algerian. Don't worry—these people here see to it that I remembor. But I'm afraid of the war you're making.
Is our house in Biskra finished? I'm longing to see it.

Your brother thinks of you,
Saïd

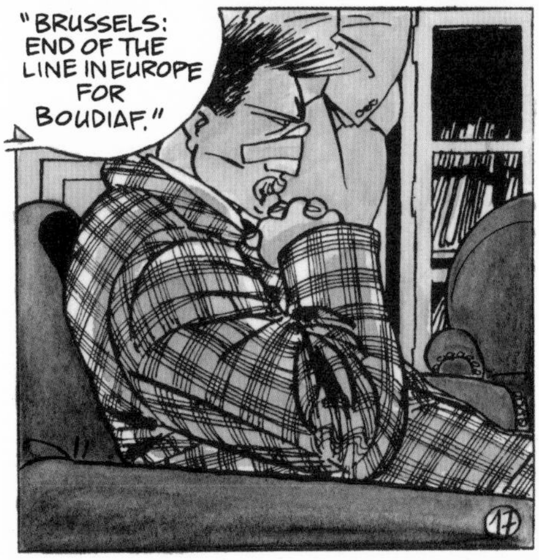
"BRUSSELS: END OF THE LINE IN EUROPE FOR BOUDIAF."

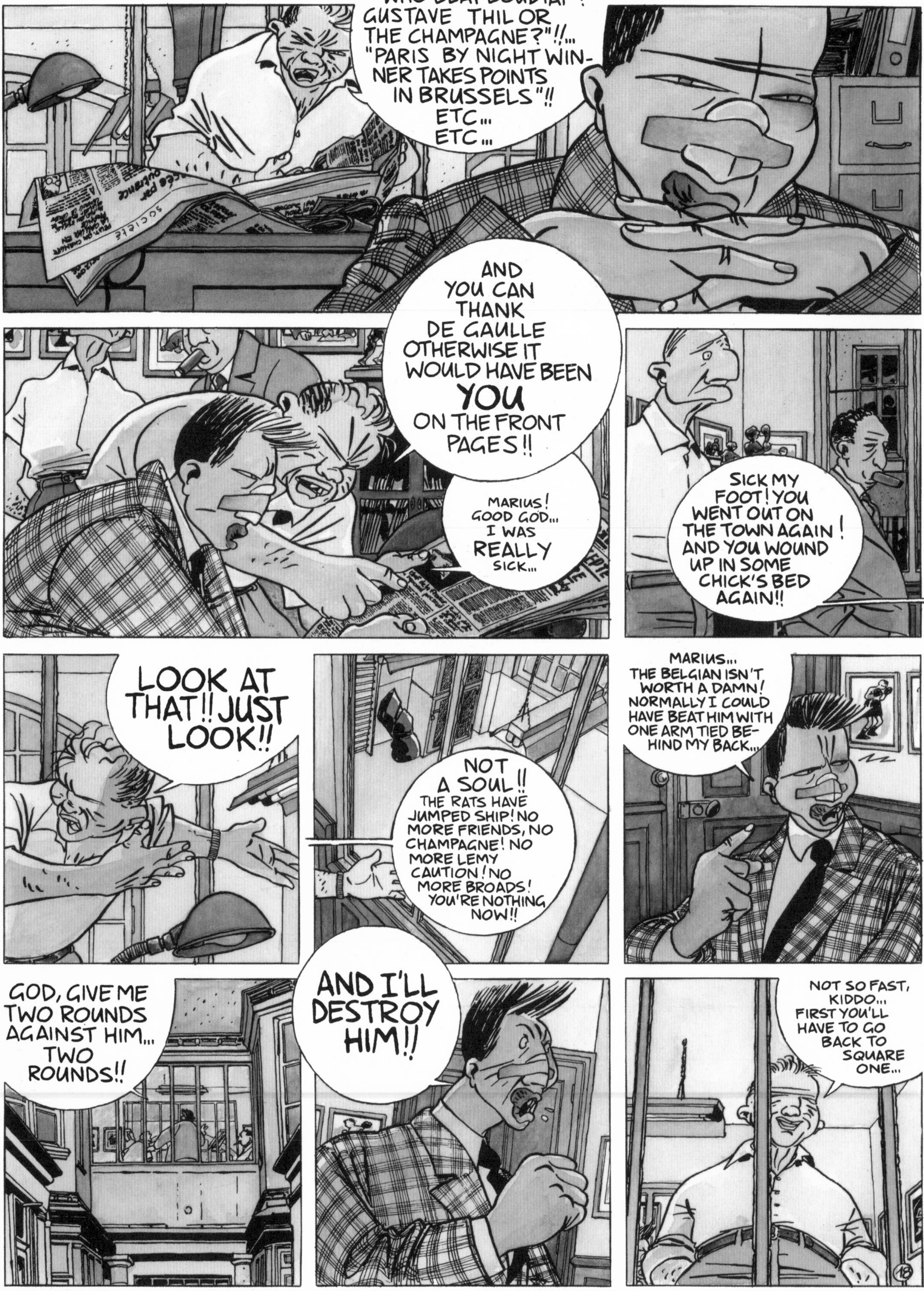
"WHO BEAT BOUDIAF? GUSTAVE THIL OR THE CHAMPAGNE?"!/... "PARIS BY NIGHT WINNER TAKES POINTS IN BRUSSELS"!! ETC... ETC...
AND YOU CAN THANK DE GAULLE OTHERWISE IT WOULD HAVE BEEN YOU ON THE FRONT PAGES!!
MARIUS! GOOD GOD... I WAS REALLY SICK...
SICK MY FOOT! YOU WENT OUT ON THE TOWN AGAIN! AND YOU WOUND UP IN SOME CHICK'S BED AGAIN!!
LOOK AT THAT!! JUST LOOK!!
NOT A SOUL!! THE RATS HAVE JUMPED SHIP! NO MORE FRIENDS, NO CHAMPAGNE! NO MORE LEMY CAUTION! NO MORE BROADS! YOU'RE NOTHING NOW!!
MARIUS... THE BELGIAN ISN'T WORTH A DAMN! NORMALLY I COULD HAVE BEAT HIM WITH ONE ARM TIED BEHIND MY BACK...
GOD, GIVE ME TWO ROUNDS AGAINST HIM... TWO ROUNDS!!
AND I'LL DESTROY HIM!!
NOT SO FAST, KIDDO... FIRST YOU'LL HAVE TO GO BACK TO SQUARE ONE...

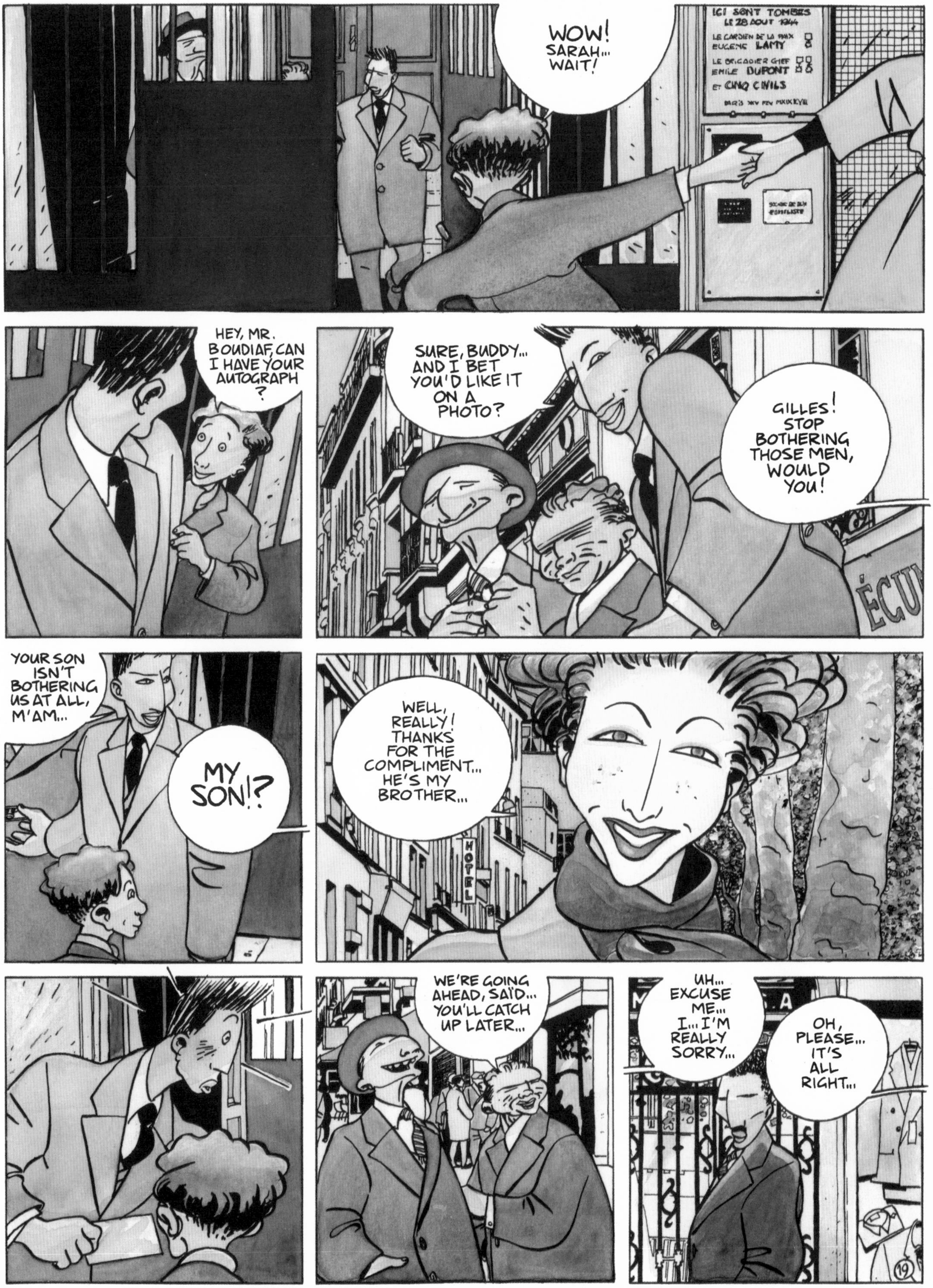
WOW! SARAH... WAIT!
ICI SONT TOMBES
LE 28 AOUT 1944
LE CARDIEN DE LA PAIX
EUGENE LAMY
LE BRIGADIER CHEF
EMILE DUPONT
ET CINQ CIVILS
HEY, MR. BOUDIAF, CAN I HAVE YOUR AUTOGRAPH?
SURE, BUDDY... AND I BET YOU'D LIKE IT ON A PHOTO?
GILLES! STOP BOTHERING THOSE MEN, WOULD YOU!
ÉCU
YOUR SON ISN'T BOTHERING US AT ALL, M'AM...
MY SON!?
WELL, REALLY! THANKS FOR THE COMPLIMENT... HE'S MY BROTHER...
HOTEL
WE'RE GOING AHEAD, SAÏD... YOU'LL CATCH UP LATER...
UH... EXCUSE ME... I... I'M REALLY SORRY...
OH, PLEASE... IT'S ALL RIGHT...

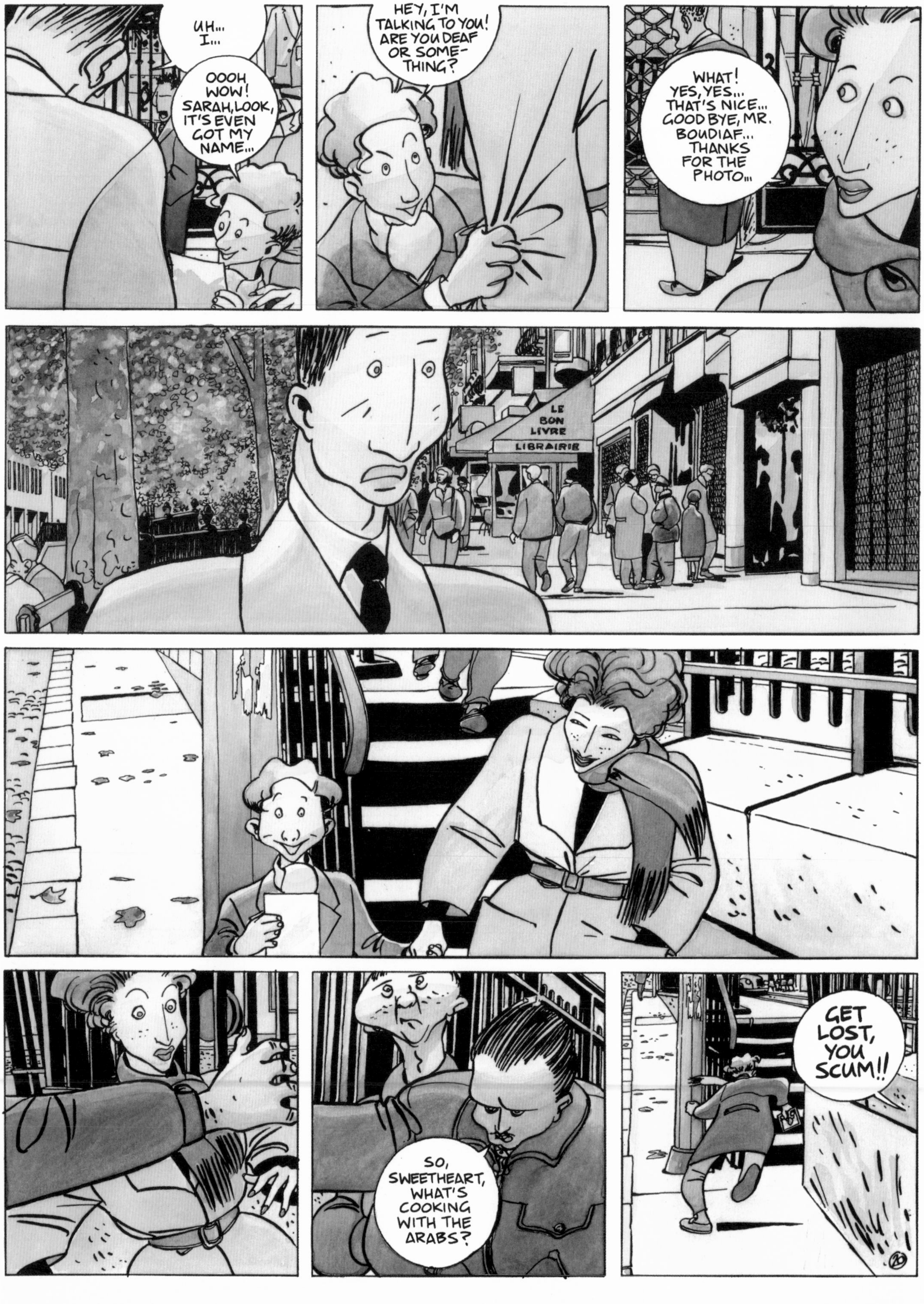
UH... I...
OOOH WOW! SARAH, LOOK, IT'S EVEN GOT MY NAME...
HEY, I'M TALKING TO YOU! ARE YOU DEAF OR SOME-THING?
WHAT! YES, YES... THAT'S NICE... GOOD BYE, MR. BOUDIAF... THANKS FOR THE PHOTO...
LE BON LIVRE
LIBRAIRIE
SO, SWEETHEART, WHAT'S COOKING WITH THE ARABS?
GET LOST, YOU SCUM!!

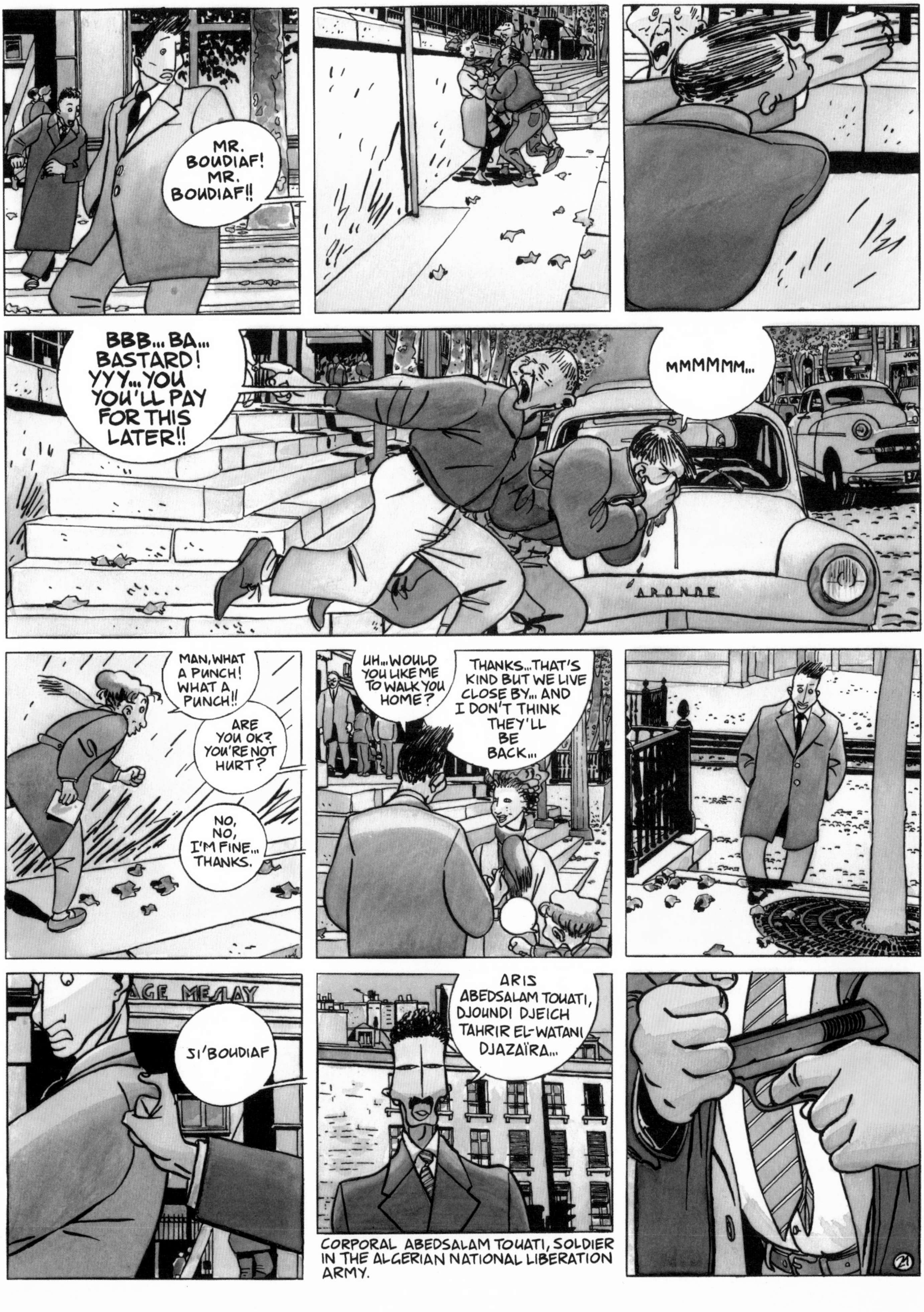
MR. BOUDIAF! MR. BOUDIAF!!
BBB... BA... BASTARD! YYY... YOU YOU'LL PAY FOR THIS LATER!!
MMMMMM...
MAN, WHAT A PUNCH! WHAT A PUNCH!!
ARE YOU OK? YOU'RE NOT HURT?
NO, NO, I'M FINE... THANKS.
UH... WOULD YOU LIKE ME TO WALK YOU HOME?
THANKS... THAT'S KIND BUT WE LIVE CLOSE BY... AND I DON'T THINK THEY'LL BE BACK...
AGE MESLAY
SI'BOUDIAF
ARIS ABEDSALAM TOUATI, DJOUNDI DJEICH TAHRIR EL-WATANI DJAZAÏRA...
CORPORAL ABEDSALAM TOUATI, SOLDIER IN THE ALGERIAN NATIONAL LIBERATION ARMY.
ARONDE

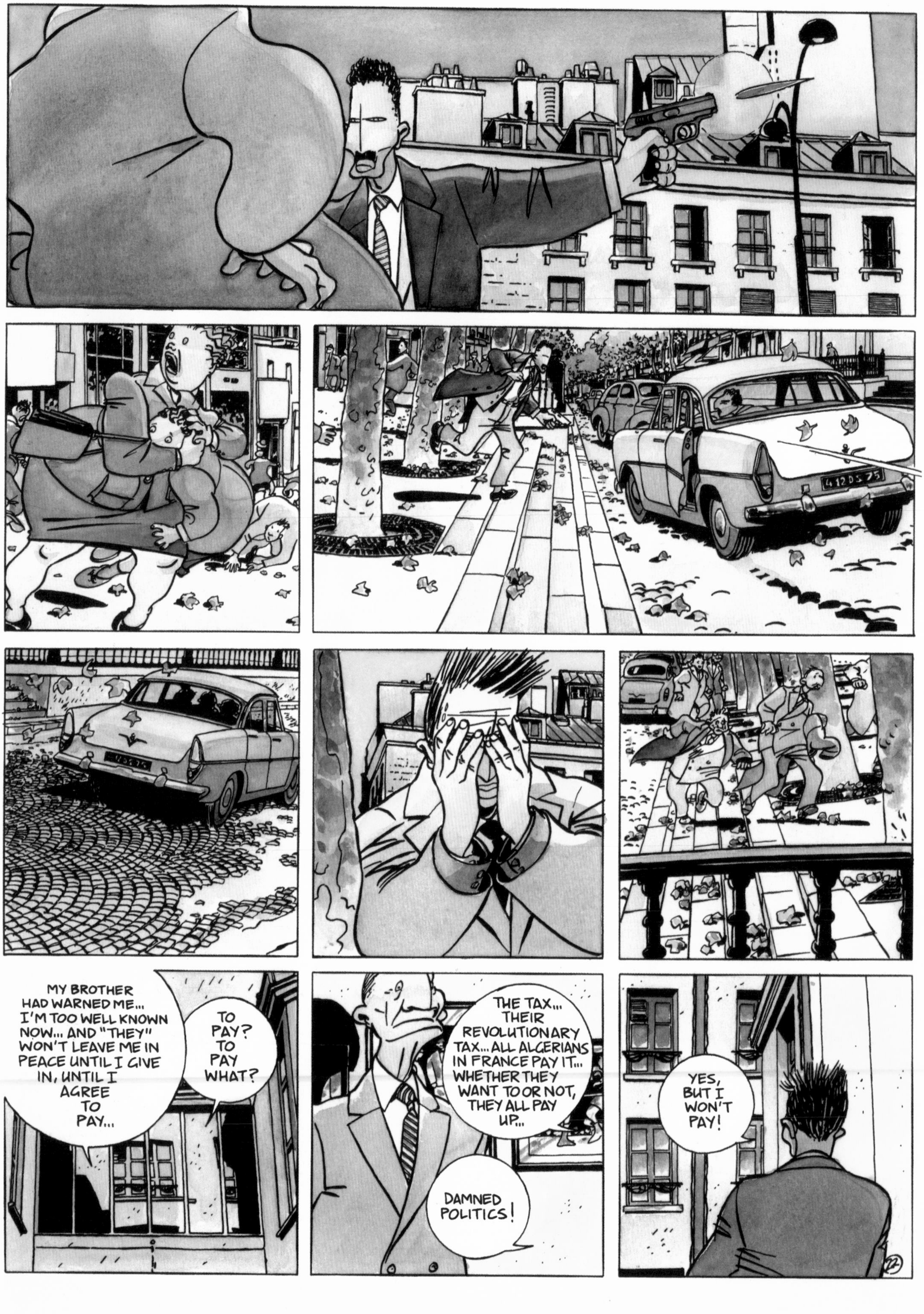
MY BROTHER HAD WARNED ME... I'M TOO WELL KNOWN NOW... AND "THEY" WON'T LEAVE ME IN PEACE UNTIL I GIVE IN, UNTIL I AGREE TO PAY...
TO PAY? TO PAY WHAT?
THE TAX... THEIR REVOLUTIONARY TAX... ALL ALGERIANS IN FRANCE PAY IT... WHETHER THEY WANT TO OR NOT, THEY ALL PAY UP...
DAMNED POLITICS!
YES, BUT I WON'T PAY!

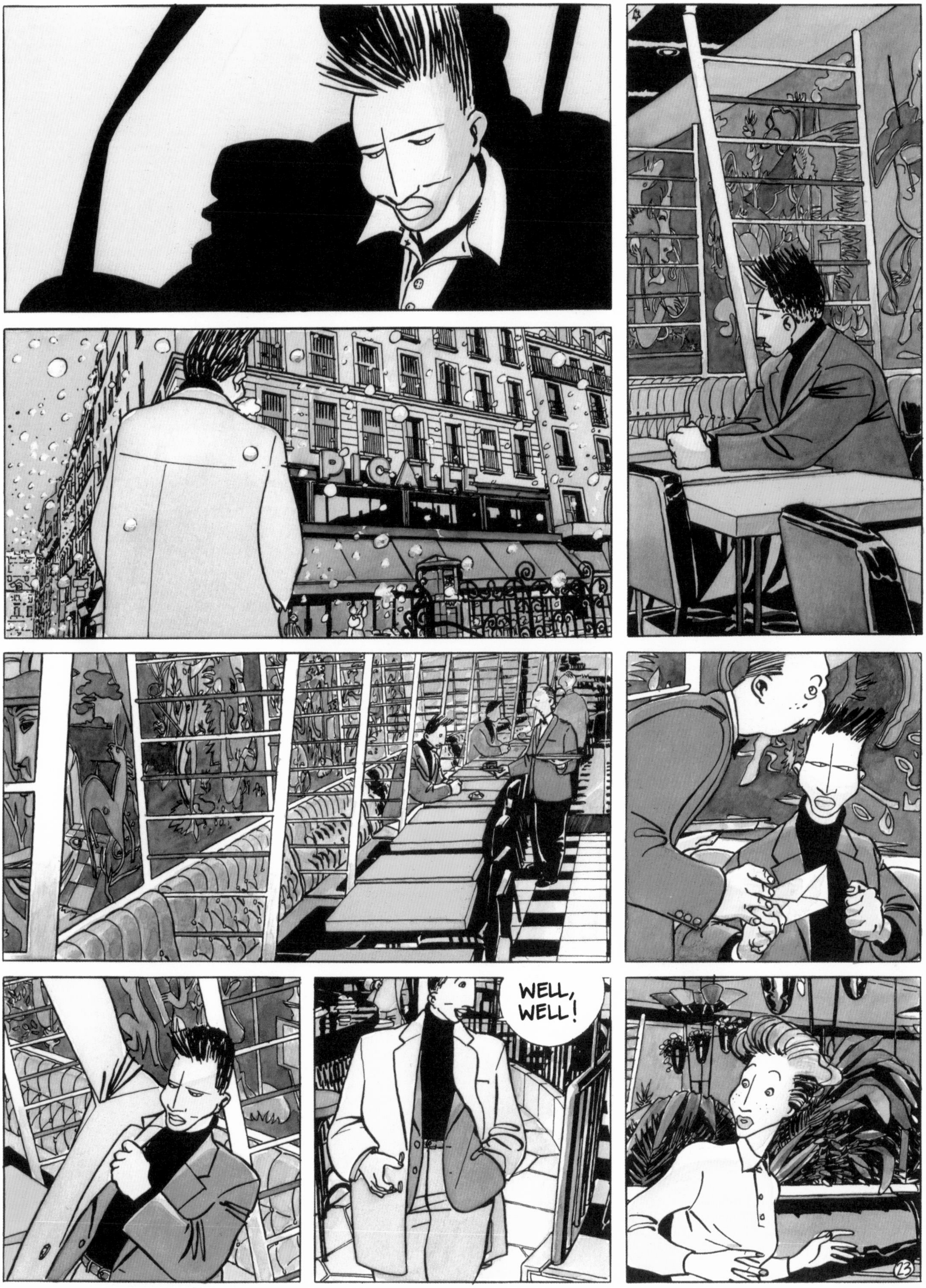
WELL, WELL!

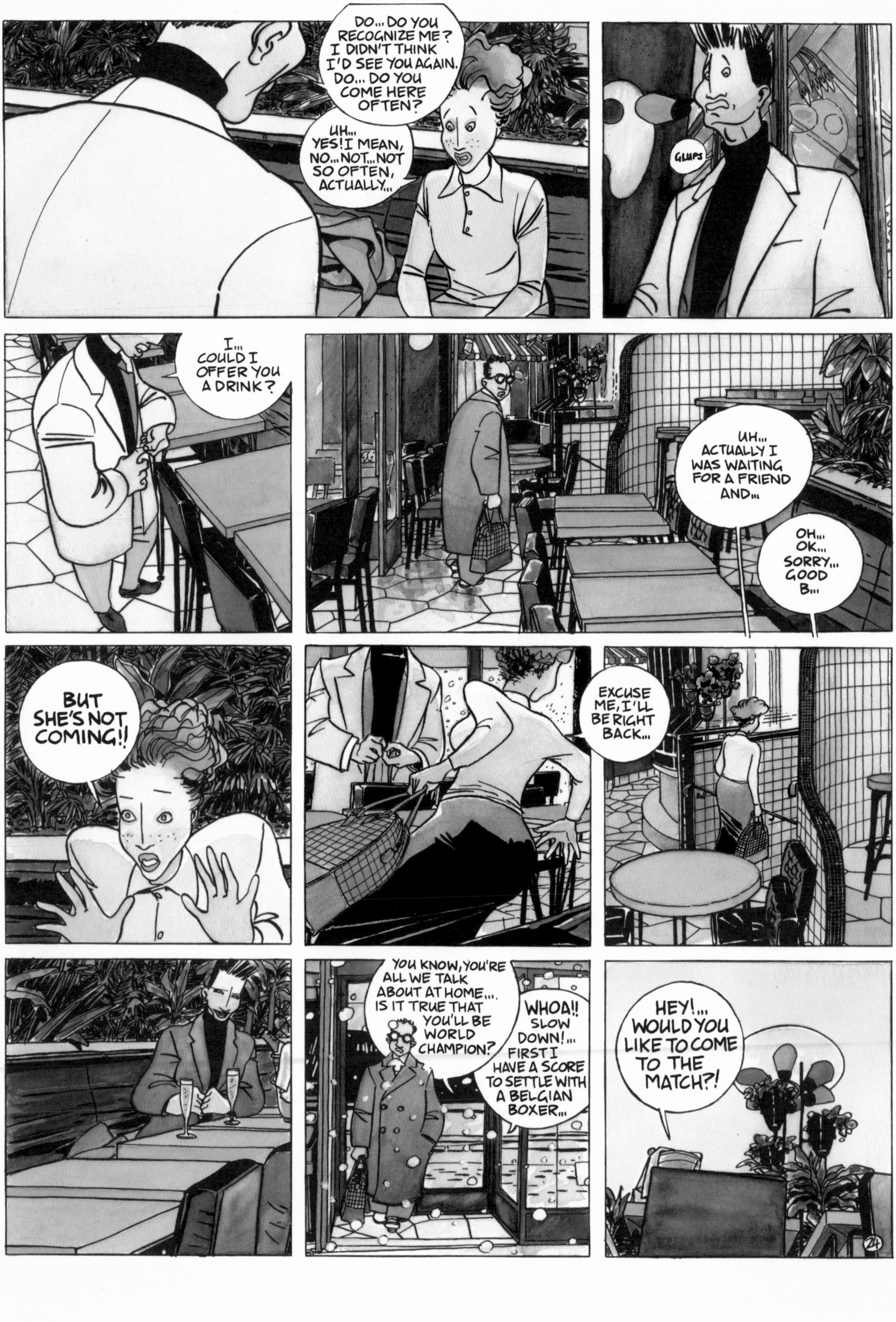
DO... DO YOU RECOGNIZE ME? I DIDN'T THINK I'D SEE YOU AGAIN. DO... DO YOU COME HERE OFTEN?
UH... YES! I MEAN, NO... NOT... NOT SO OFTEN, ACTUALLY...
GLUPS
I... COULD I OFFER YOU A DRINK?
UH... ACTUALLY I WAS WAITING FOR A FRIEND AND...
OH... OK... SORRY... GOOD B...
BUT SHE'S NOT COMING!!
EXCUSE ME, I'LL BE RIGHT BACK...
YOU KNOW, YOU'RE ALL WE TALK ABOUT AT HOME... IS IT TRUE THAT YOU'LL BE WORLD CHAMPION?
WHOA!! SLOW DOWN!... FIRST I HAVE A SCORE TO SETTLE WITH A BELGIAN BOXER...
HEY!... WOULD YOU LIKE TO COME TO THE MATCH?!
24

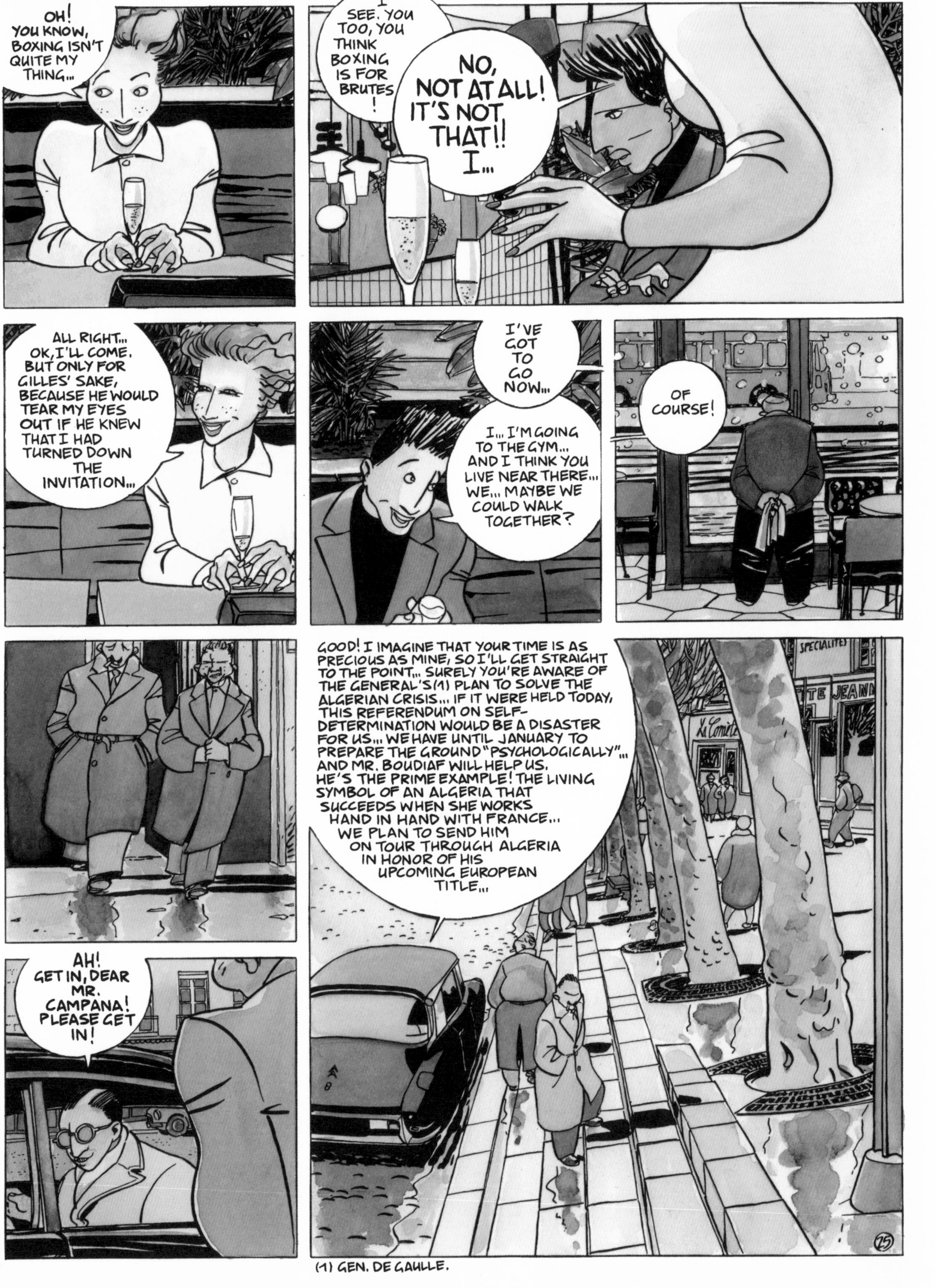
OH! YOU KNOW, BOXING ISN'T QUITE MY THING...
I SEE. YOU TOO, YOU THINK BOXING IS FOR BRUTES!
NO, NOT AT ALL! IT'S NOT THAT!! I...
ALL RIGHT... OK, I'LL COME. BUT ONLY FOR GILLES' SAKE, BECAUSE HE WOULD TEAR MY EYES OUT IF HE KNEW THAT I HAD TURNED DOWN THE INVITATION...
I'VE GOT TO GO NOW...
I... I'M GOING TO THE GYM... AND I THINK YOU LIVE NEAR THERE... WE... MAYBE WE COULD WALK TOGETHER?
OF COURSE!
GOOD! I IMAGINE THAT YOUR TIME IS AS PRECIOUS AS MINE, SO I'LL GET STRAIGHT TO THE POINT... SURELY YOU'RE AWARE OF THE GENERAL'S(1) PLAN TO SOLVE THE ALGERIAN CRISIS... IF IT WERE HELD TODAY, THIS REFERENDUM ON SELF-DETERMINATION WOULD BE A DISASTER FOR US... WE HAVE UNTIL JANUARY TO PREPARE THE GROUND "PSYCHOLOGICALLY"... AND MR. BOUDIAF WILL HELP US. HE'S THE PRIME EXAMPLE! THE LIVING SYMBOL OF AN ALGERIA THAT SUCCEEDS WHEN SHE WORKS HAND IN HAND WITH FRANCE... WE PLAN TO SEND HIM ON TOUR THROUGH ALGERIA IN HONOR OF HIS UPCOMING EUROPEAN TITLE...
SPECIALITES
AH! GET IN, DEAR MR. CAMPANA! PLEASE GET IN!

(1) GEN. DE GAULLE.

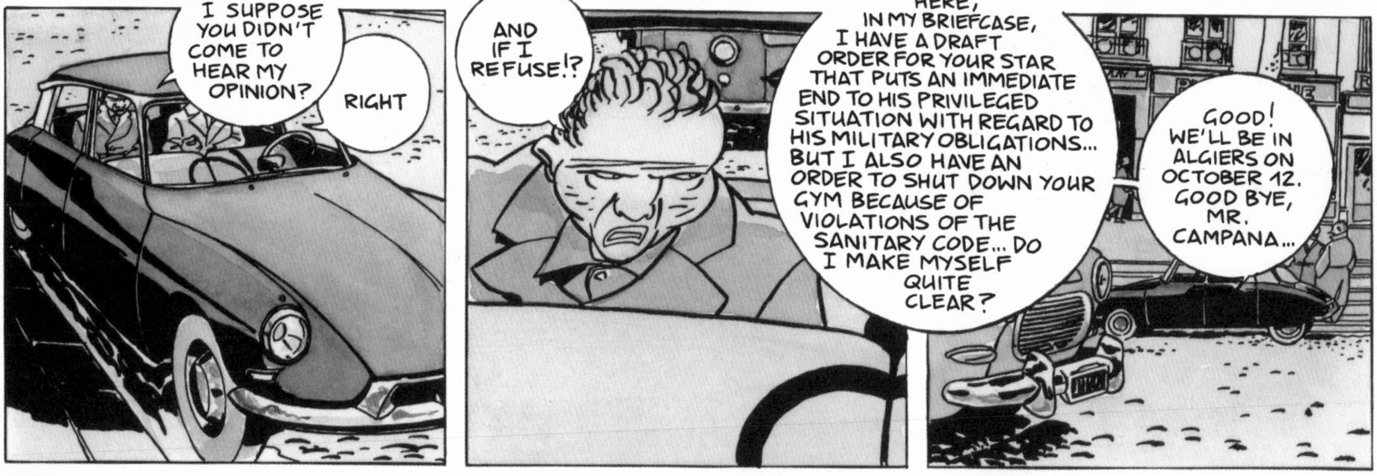
I SUPPOSE YOU DIDN'T COME TO HEAR MY OPINION?
RIGHT
AND IF I REFUSE!?
HERE, IN MY BRIEFCASE, I HAVE A DRAFT ORDER FOR YOUR STAR THAT PUTS AN IMMEDIATE END TO HIS PRIVILEGED SITUATION WITH REGARD TO HIS MILITARY OBLIGATIONS... BUT I ALSO HAVE AN ORDER TO SHUT DOWN YOUR GYM BECAUSE OF VIOLATIONS OF THE SANITARY CODE... DO I MAKE MYSELF QUITE CLEAR?
GOOD! WE'LL BE IN ALGIERS ON OCTOBER 12. GOOD BYE, MR. CAMPANA...

Saïd Boudiaf-Gustave Thil

PLACE: *PALAIS DES SPORTS, PARIS*
DATE: *JULY 4, 1959*
ATTENDANCE: 12,741

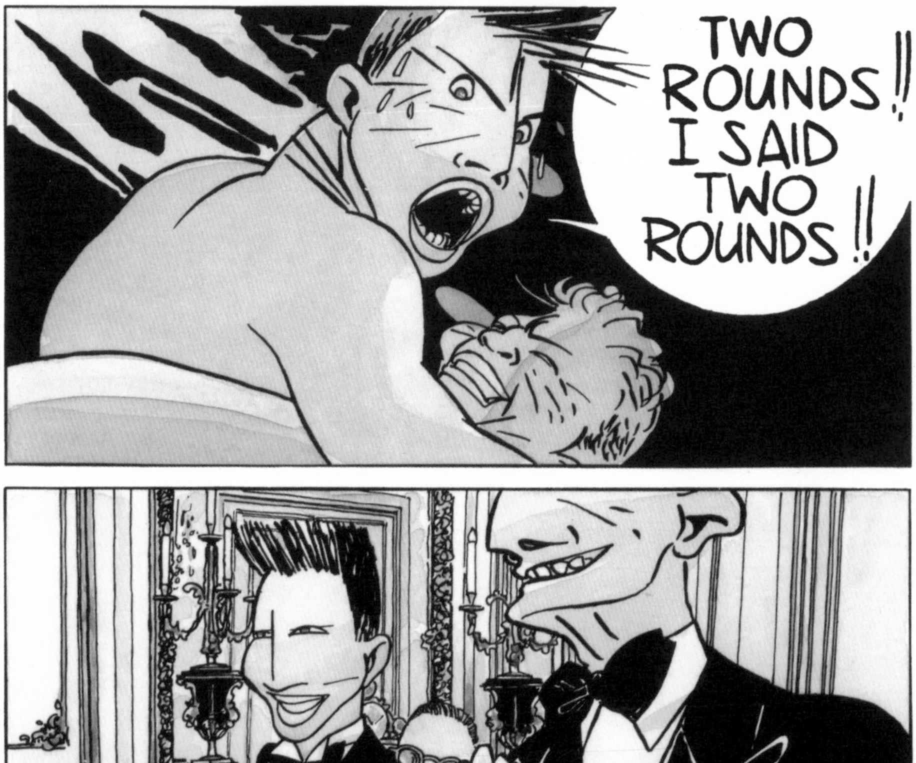
TWO ROUNDS!! I SAID TWO ROUNDS!!

1st Round

OVER-CONFIDENT? WHATEVER THE CASE, EUROPE'S CHAMPION APPROACHES BOUDIAF WITH HIS GUARD DOWN. HE SIDESTEPS A SHARP RIGHT HOOK BUT NOT THE LEFT THAT FOLLOWS. HE COLLAPSES. "ONE!" HE'S UP. ANOTHER RIGHT. GUSTAVE THIL IS CATAPULTED INTO THE CORDS. BOUDIAF IS ON HIM AND DELIVERS A SERIES OF LETHAL HOOKS. THIL CLINCHES. BOUDIAF PULLS AWAY AND CONTINUES THE ASSAULT. THIL TRIES A LARGE LEFT SWING. BOUDIAF ANSWERS WITH A LEFT HOOK AND A SHORT, DRY RIGHT ON THE CHIN. DAZED, THIL FALLS FLAT ON HIS BACK, HIS ARMS OUT WIDE. SAÏD BOUDIAF IS THE EUROPEAN CHAMPION. THE FIGHT LASTED 132 SECONDS.

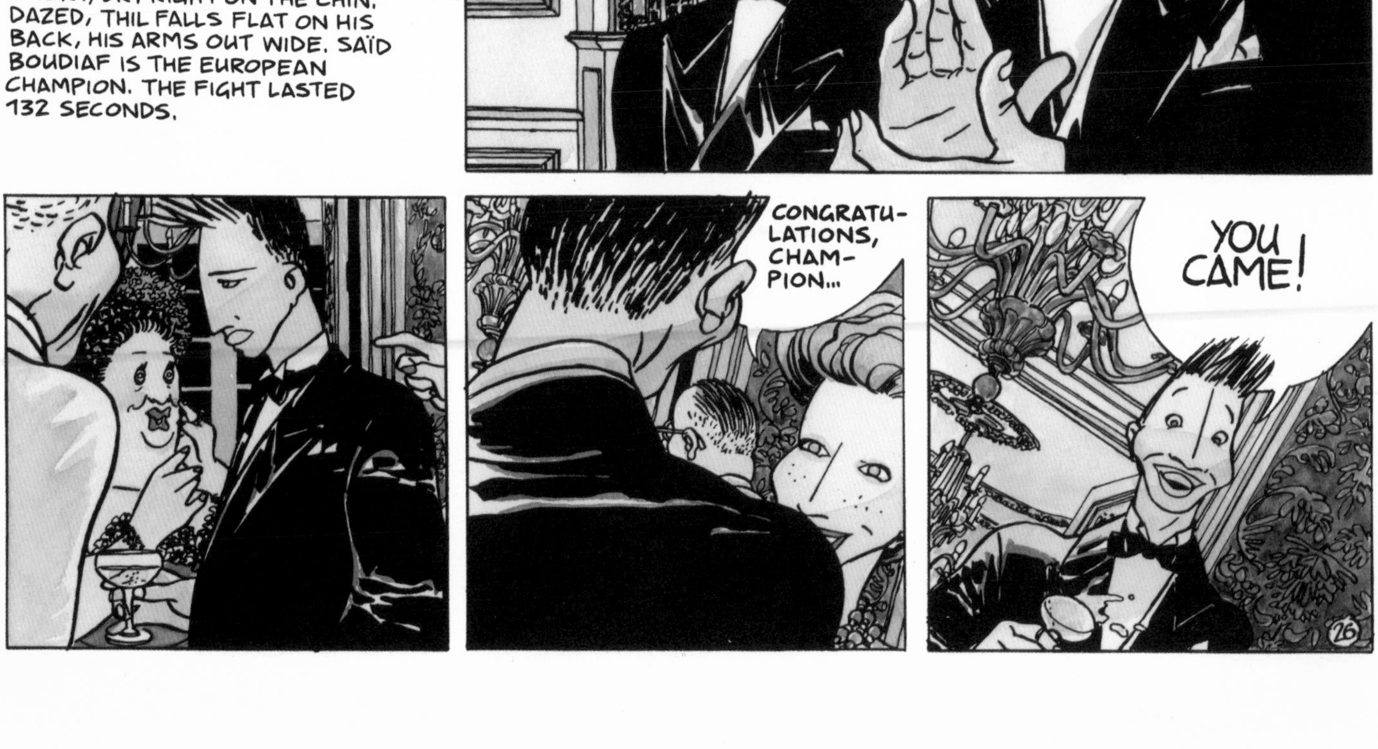
CONGRATULATIONS, CHAMPION...
YOU CAME!

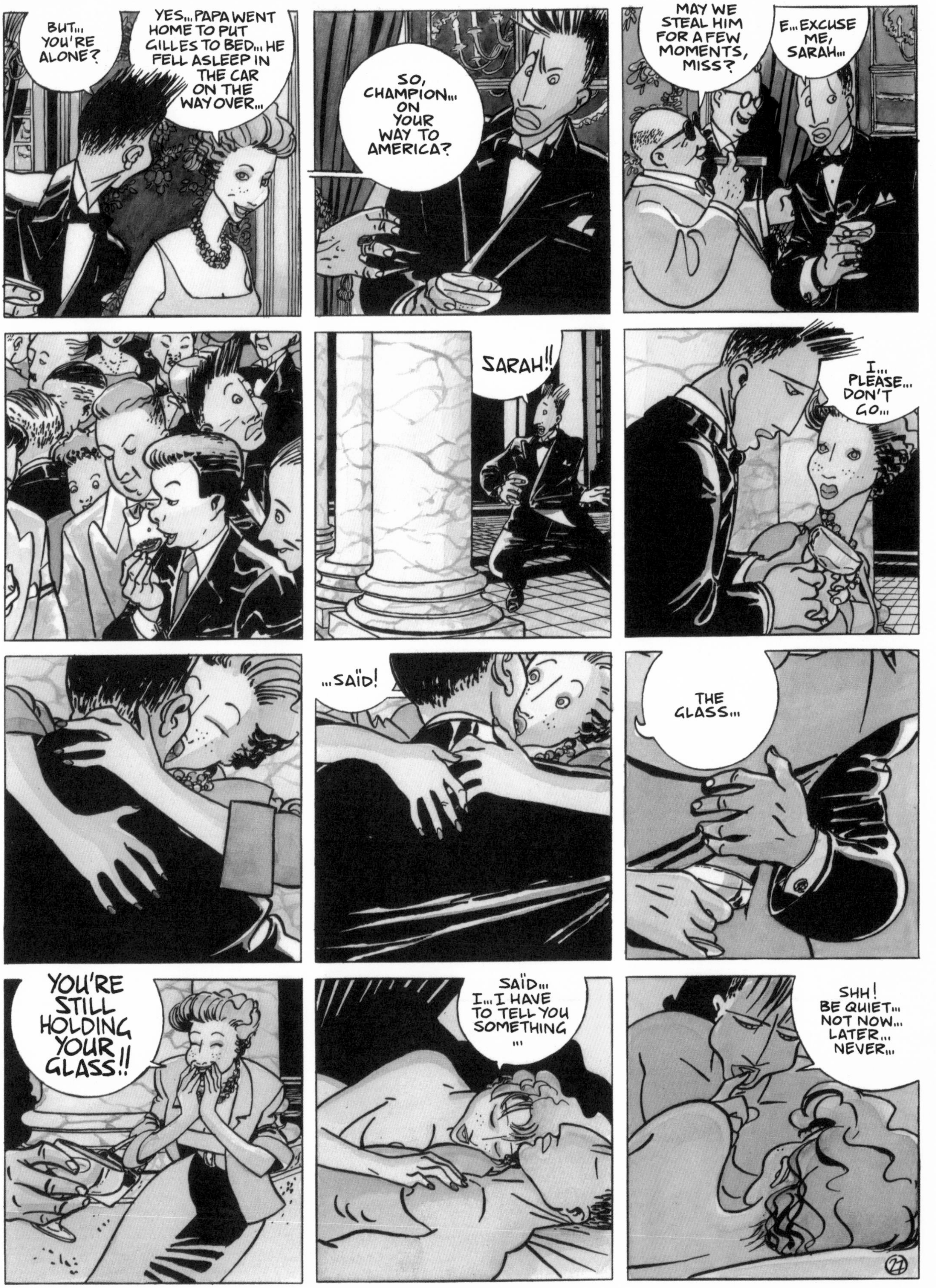
BUT... YOU'RE ALONE?
YES... PAPA WENT HOME TO PUT GILLES TO BED... HE FELL ASLEEP IN THE CAR ON THE WAY OVER...
SO, CHAMPION... ON YOUR WAY TO AMERICA?
MAY WE STEAL HIM FOR A FEW MOMENTS, MISS?
E... EXCUSE ME, SARAH...
SARAH!!
I... PLEASE... DON'T GO...
...SAÏD!
THE GLASS...
YOU'RE STILL HOLDING YOUR GLASS!!
SAÏD... I... I HAVE TO TELL YOU SOMETHING ...
SHH! BE QUIET... NOT NOW... LATER... NEVER...
27

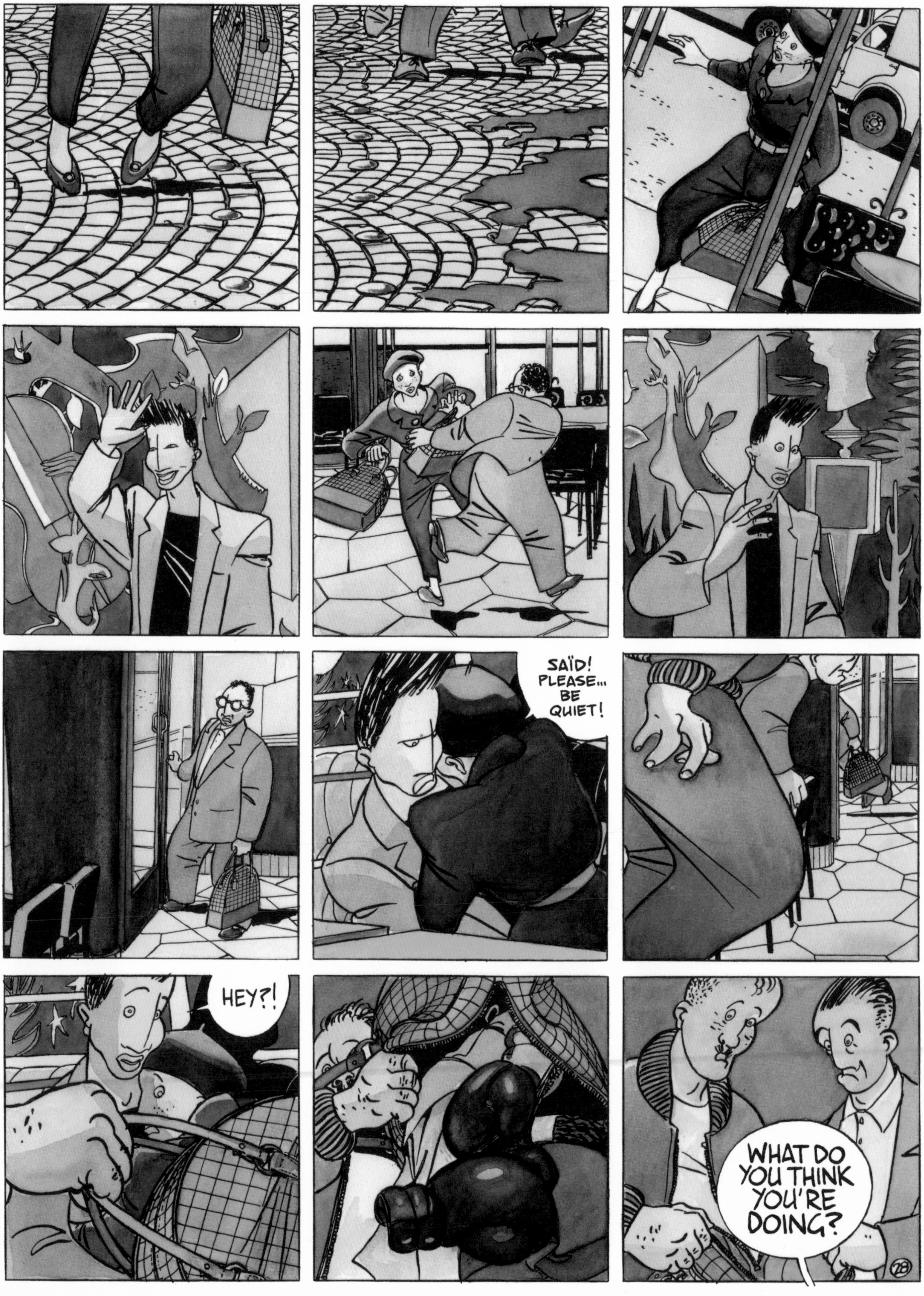
SAÏD! PLEASE... BE QUIET!
HEY?!
WHAT DO YOU THINK YOU'RE DOING?
28

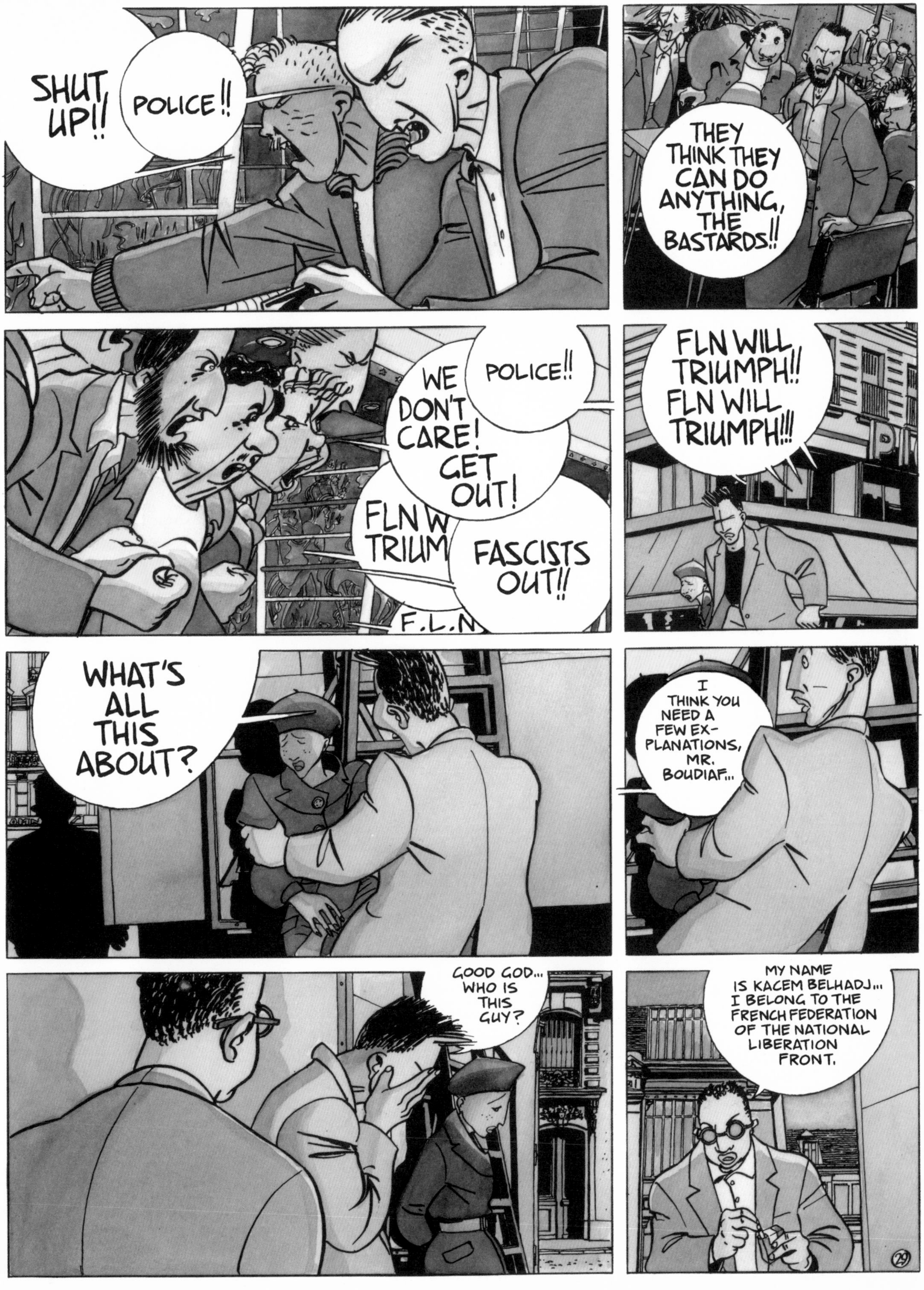
SHUT UP!!
POLICE!!
THEY THINK THEY CAN DO ANYTHING, THE BASTARDS!!
WE DON'T CARE! GET OUT!
POLICE!!
FLN W TRIUM
FASCISTS OUT!!
F.L.N
FLN WILL TRIUMPH!! FLN WILL TRIUMPH!!!
WHAT'S ALL THIS ABOUT?
I THINK YOU NEED A FEW EX-PLANATIONS, MR. BOUDIAF...
GOOD GOD... WHO IS THIS GUY?
MY NAME IS KACEM BELHADJ... I BELONG TO THE FRENCH FEDERATION OF THE NATIONAL LIBERATION FRONT.

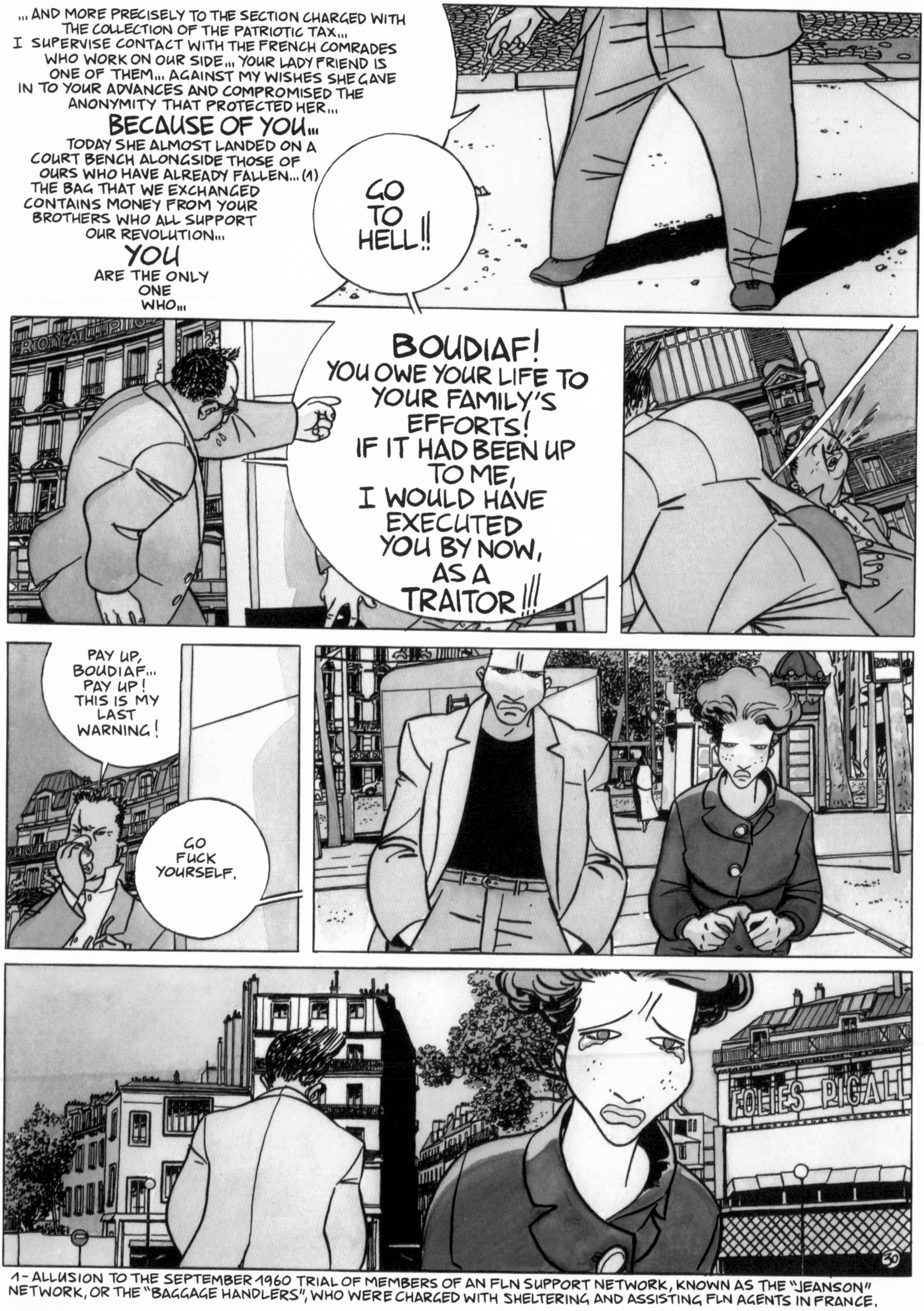
...AND MORE PRECISELY TO THE SECTION CHARGED WITH THE COLLECTION OF THE PATRIOTIC TAX... I SUPERVISE CONTACT WITH THE FRENCH COMRADES WHO WORK ON OUR SIDE... YOUR LADY FRIEND IS ONE OF THEM... AGAINST MY WISHES SHE GAVE IN TO YOUR ADVANCES AND COMPROMISED THE ANONYMITY THAT PROTECTED HER... BECAUSE OF YOU... TODAY SHE ALMOST LANDED ON A COURT BENCH ALONGSIDE THOSE OF OURS WHO HAVE ALREADY FALLEN... (1) THE BAG THAT WE EXCHANGED CONTAINS MONEY FROM YOUR BROTHERS WHO ALL SUPPORT OUR REVOLUTION... YOU ARE THE ONLY ONE WHO...
GO TO HELL!!
BOUDIAF! YOU OWE YOUR LIFE TO YOUR FAMILY'S EFFORTS! IF IT HAD BEEN UP TO ME, I WOULD HAVE EXECUTED YOU BY NOW, AS A TRAITOR!!!
PAY UP, BOUDIAF... PAY UP! THIS IS MY LAST WARNING!
GO FUCK YOURSELF.
FOLIES PIGALL
30

1- ALLUSION TO THE SEPTEMBER 1960 TRIAL OF MEMBERS OF AN FLN SUPPORT NETWORK, KNOWN AS THE "JEANSON" NETWORK, OR THE "BAGGAGE HANDLERS", WHO WERE CHARGED WITH SHELTERING AND ASSISTING FLN AGENTS IN FRANCE.

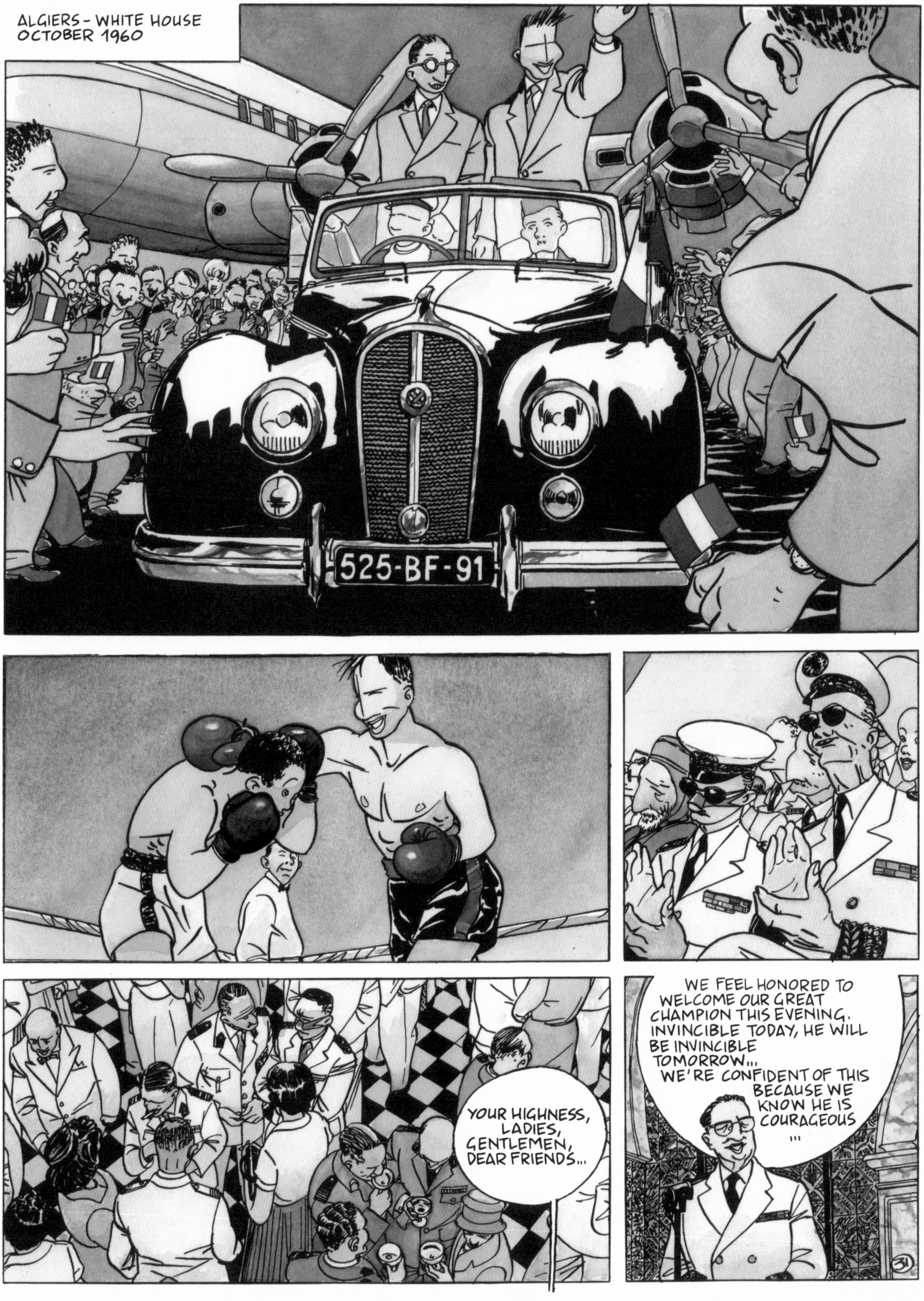
ALGIERS - WHITE HOUSE
OCTOBER 1960
525-BF-91
YOUR HIGHNESS, LADIES, GENTLEMEN, DEAR FRIENDS...
WE FEEL HONORED TO WELCOME OUR GREAT CHAMPION THIS EVENING. INVINCIBLE TODAY, HE WILL BE INVINCIBLE TOMORROW... WE'RE CONFIDENT OF THIS BECAUSE WE KNOW HE IS COURAGEOUS ...

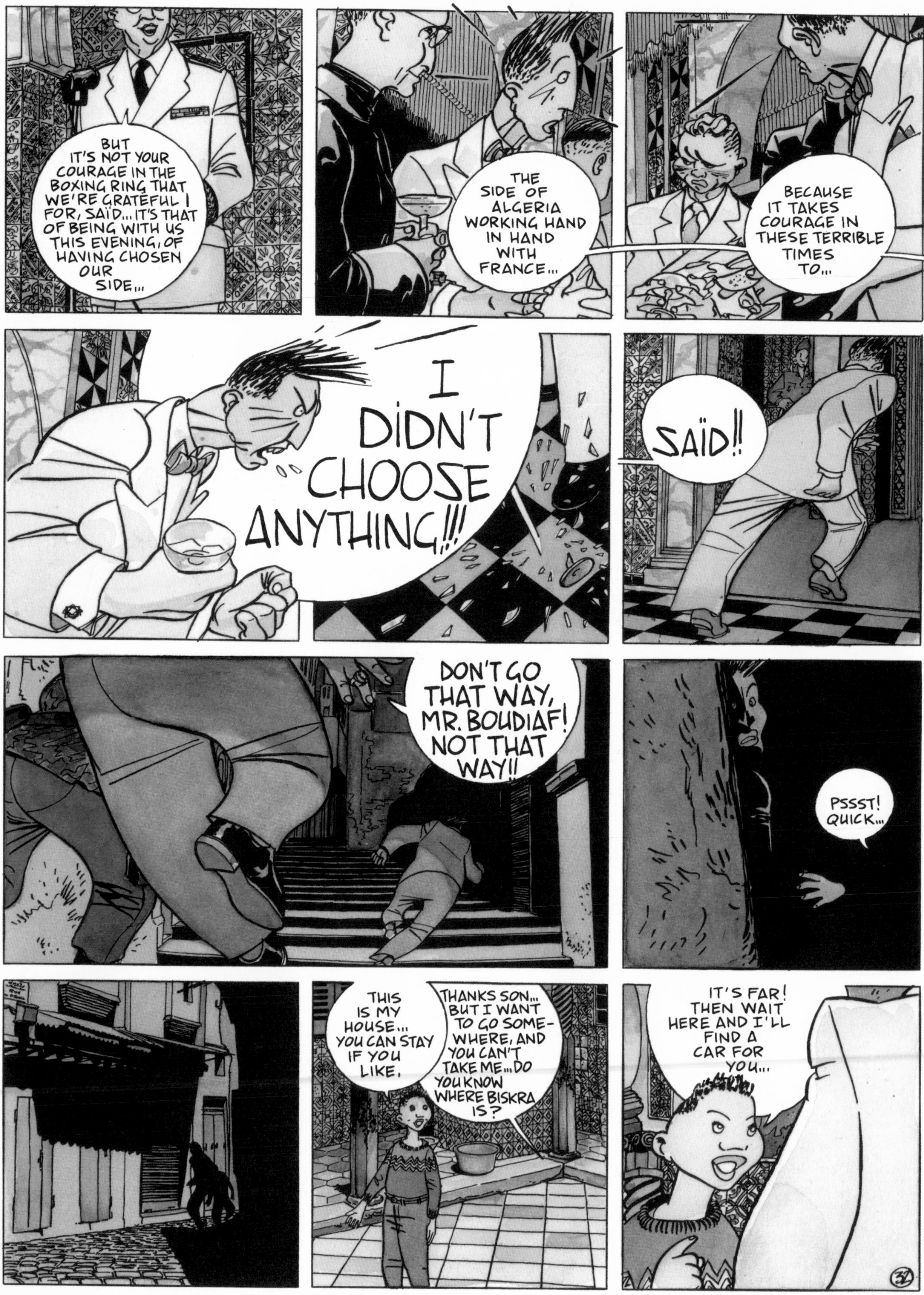

BUT IT'S NOT YOUR COURAGE IN THE BOXING RING THAT WE'RE GRATEFUL FOR, SAÏD... IT'S THAT OF BEING WITH US THIS EVENING, OF HAVING CHOSEN OUR SIDE...
THE SIDE OF ALGERIA WORKING HAND IN HAND WITH FRANCE...
BECAUSE IT TAKES COURAGE IN THESE TERRIBLE TIMES TO...
I DIDN'T CHOOSE ANYTHING!!!
SAÏD!!
DON'T GO THAT WAY, MR. BOUDIAF! NOT THAT WAY!!
PSSST! QUICK...
THIS IS MY HOUSE... YOU CAN STAY IF YOU LIKE.
THANKS SON... BUT I WANT TO GO SOMEWHERE, AND YOU CAN'T TAKE ME... DO YOU KNOW WHERE BISKRA IS?
IT'S FAR! THEN WAIT HERE AND I'LL FIND A CAR FOR YOU...

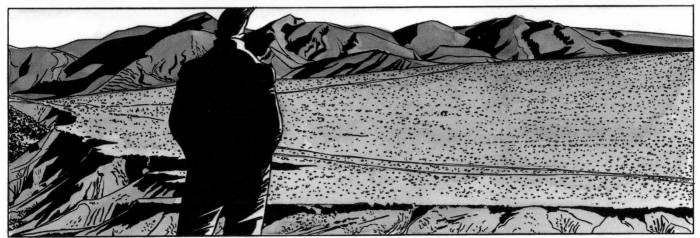

THEY HARDLY LIVED HERE AT ALL, YOU KNOW... I HAD TO BRING THEM TO SAFETY IN TUNISIA...

33

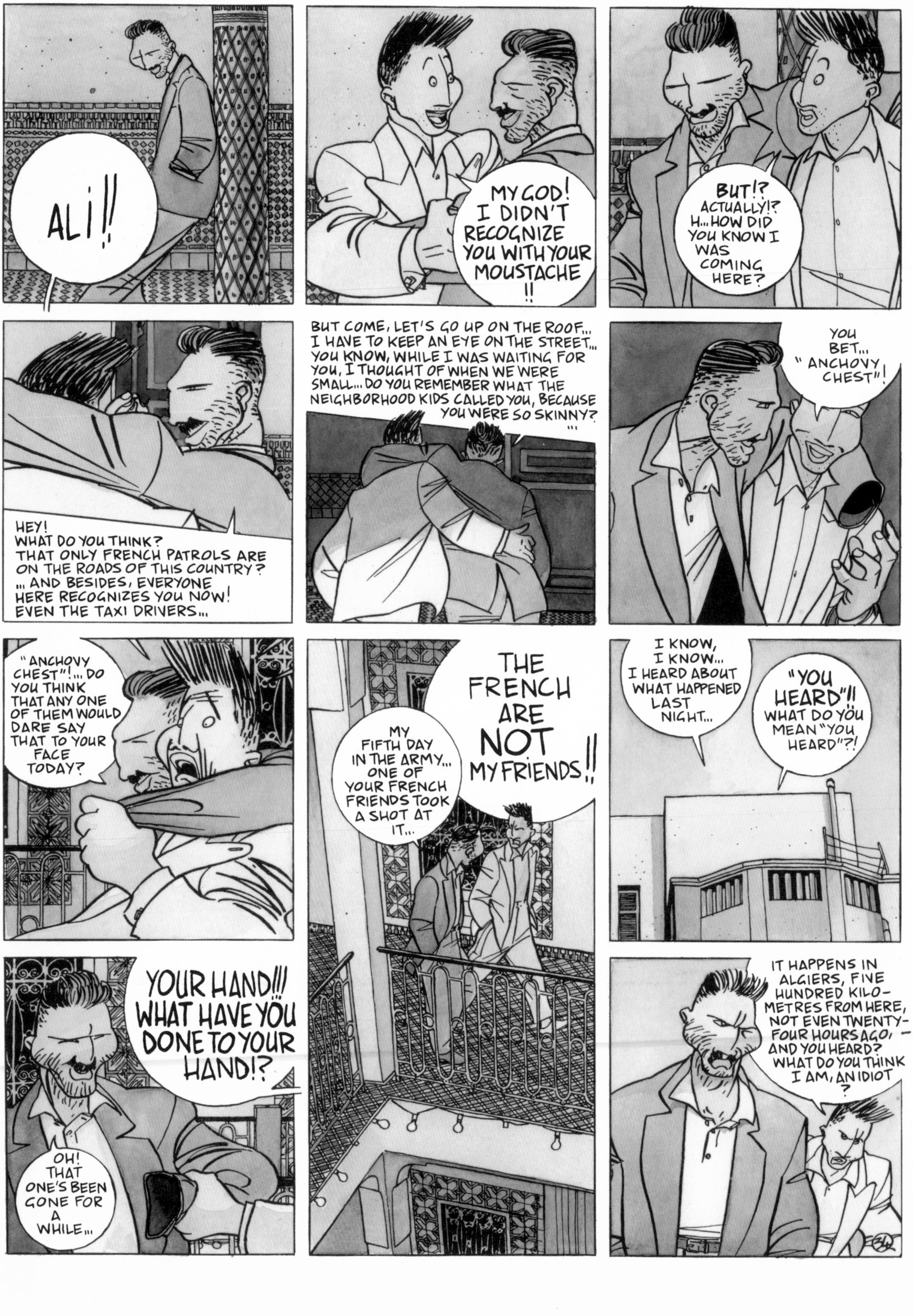
ALI!!
MY GOD! I DIDN'T RECOGNIZE YOU WITH YOUR MOUSTACHE!!
BUT!? ACTUALLY!? H... HOW DID YOU KNOW I WAS COMING HERE?
HEY! WHAT DO YOU THINK? THAT ONLY FRENCH PATROLS ARE ON THE ROADS OF THIS COUNTRY? ... AND BESIDES, EVERYONE HERE RECOGNIZES YOU NOW! EVEN THE TAXI DRIVERS...
BUT COME, LET'S GO UP ON THE ROOF... I HAVE TO KEEP AN EYE ON THE STREET... YOU KNOW, WHILE I WAS WAITING FOR YOU, I THOUGHT OF WHEN WE WERE SMALL... DO YOU REMEMBER WHAT THE NEIGHBORHOOD KIDS CALLED YOU, BECAUSE YOU WERE SO SKINNY?
...
YOU BET... "ANCHOVY CHEST"!
"ANCHOVY CHEST"!... DO YOU THINK THAT ANY ONE OF THEM WOULD DARE SAY THAT TO YOUR FACE TODAY?
MY FIFTH DAY IN THE ARMY... ONE OF YOUR FRENCH FRIENDS TOOK A SHOT AT IT...
THE FRENCH ARE NOT MY FRIENDS!!
I KNOW, I KNOW... I HEARD ABOUT WHAT HAPPENED LAST NIGHT...
"YOU HEARD"!! WHAT DO YOU MEAN "YOU HEARD"?!
YOUR HAND!!! WHAT HAVE YOU DONE TO YOUR HAND!?
OH! THAT ONE'S BEEN GONE FOR A WHILE...
IT HAPPENS IN ALGIERS, FIVE HUNDRED KILO-METRES FROM HERE, NOT EVEN TWENTY-FOUR HOURS AGO, - AND YOU HEARD? WHAT DO YOU THINK I AM, AN IDIOT?

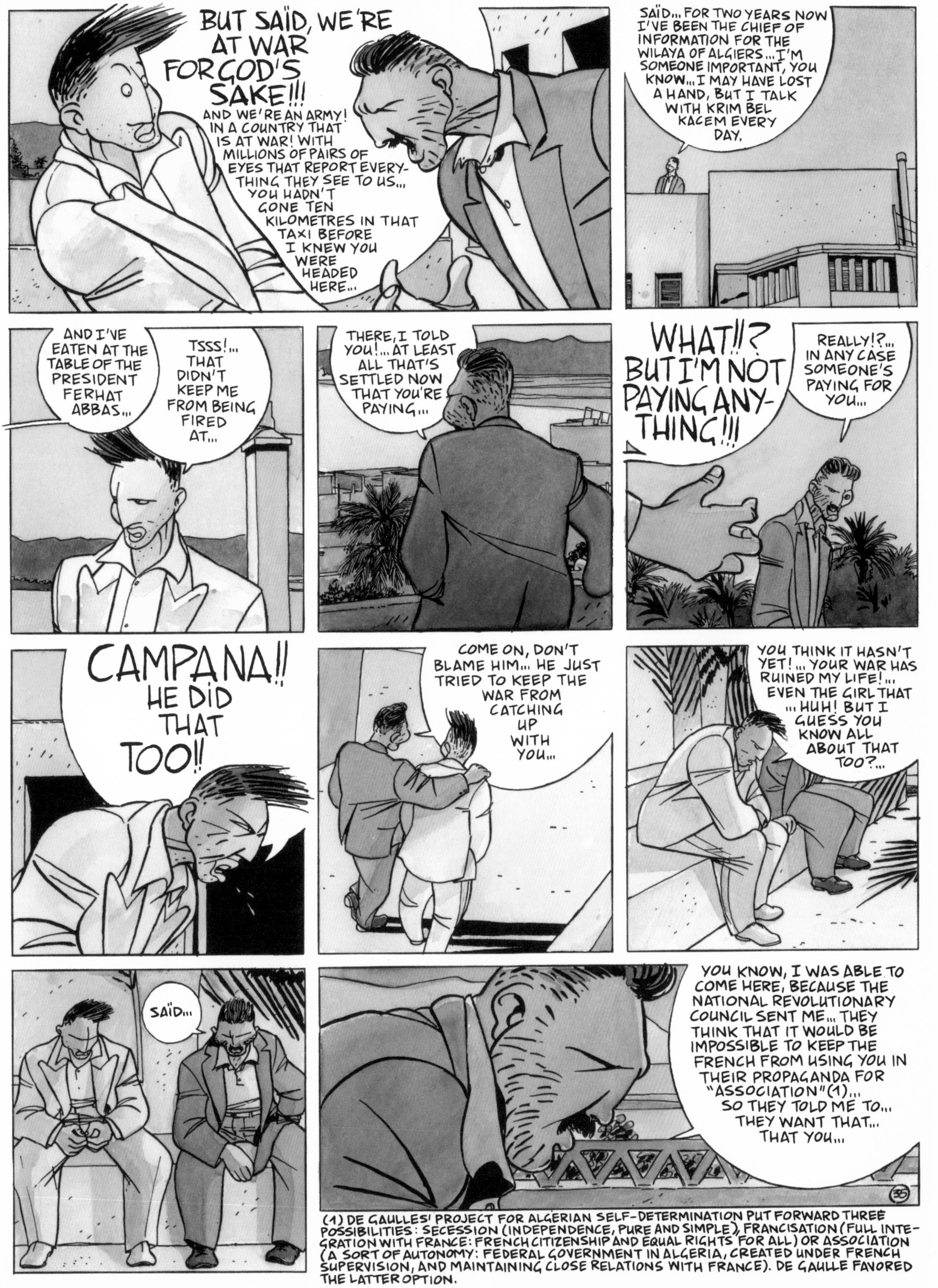

BUT SAÏD, WE'RE AT WAR FOR GOD'S SAKE!!!
AND WE'RE AN ARMY! IN A COUNTRY THAT IS AT WAR! WITH MILLIONS OF PAIRS OF EYES THAT REPORT EVERYTHING THEY SEE TO US... YOU HADN'T GONE TEN KILOMETRES IN THAT TAXI BEFORE I KNEW YOU WERE HEADED HERE...
SAÏD... FOR TWO YEARS NOW I'VE BEEN THE CHIEF OF INFORMATION FOR THE WILAYA OF ALGIERS... I'M SOMEONE IMPORTANT, YOU KNOW... I MAY HAVE LOST A HAND, BUT I TALK WITH KRIM BEL KACEM EVERY DAY.
AND I'VE EATEN AT THE TABLE OF THE PRESIDENT FERHAT ABBAS...
TSSS!... THAT DIDN'T KEEP ME FROM BEING FIRED AT...
THERE, I TOLD YOU!... AT LEAST ALL THAT'S SETTLED NOW THAT YOU'RE PAYING...
WHAT!!? BUT I'M NOT PAYING ANYTHING!!!
REALLY!?... IN ANY CASE SOMEONE'S PAYING FOR YOU...
CAMPANA!! HE DID THAT TOO!!
COME ON, DON'T BLAME HIM... HE JUST TRIED TO KEEP THE WAR FROM CATCHING UP WITH YOU...
YOU THINK IT HASN'T YET! ... YOUR WAR HAS RUINED MY LIFE!... EVEN THE GIRL THAT ... HUH! BUT I GUESS YOU KNOW ALL ABOUT THAT TOO?...
SAÏD...
YOU KNOW, I WAS ABLE TO COME HERE, BECAUSE THE NATIONAL REVOLUTIONARY COUNCIL SENT ME... THEY THINK THAT IT WOULD BE IMPOSSIBLE TO KEEP THE FRENCH FROM USING YOU IN THEIR PROPAGANDA FOR "ASSOCIATION"(1)... SO THEY TOLD ME TO... THEY WANT THAT... THAT YOU...
35

(1) DE GAULLES' PROJECT FOR ALGERIAN SELF-DETERMINATION PUT FORWARD THREE POSSIBILITIES: SECESSION (INDEPENDENCE, PURE AND SIMPLE), FRANCISATION (FULL INTEGRATION WITH FRANCE: FRENCH CITIZENSHIP AND EQUAL RIGHTS FOR ALL) OR ASSOCIATION (A SORT OF AUTONOMY: FEDERAL GOVERNMENT IN ALGERIA, CREATED UNDER FRENCH SUPERVISION, AND MAINTAINING CLOSE RELATIONS WITH FRANCE). DE GAULLE FAVORED THE LATTER OPTION.

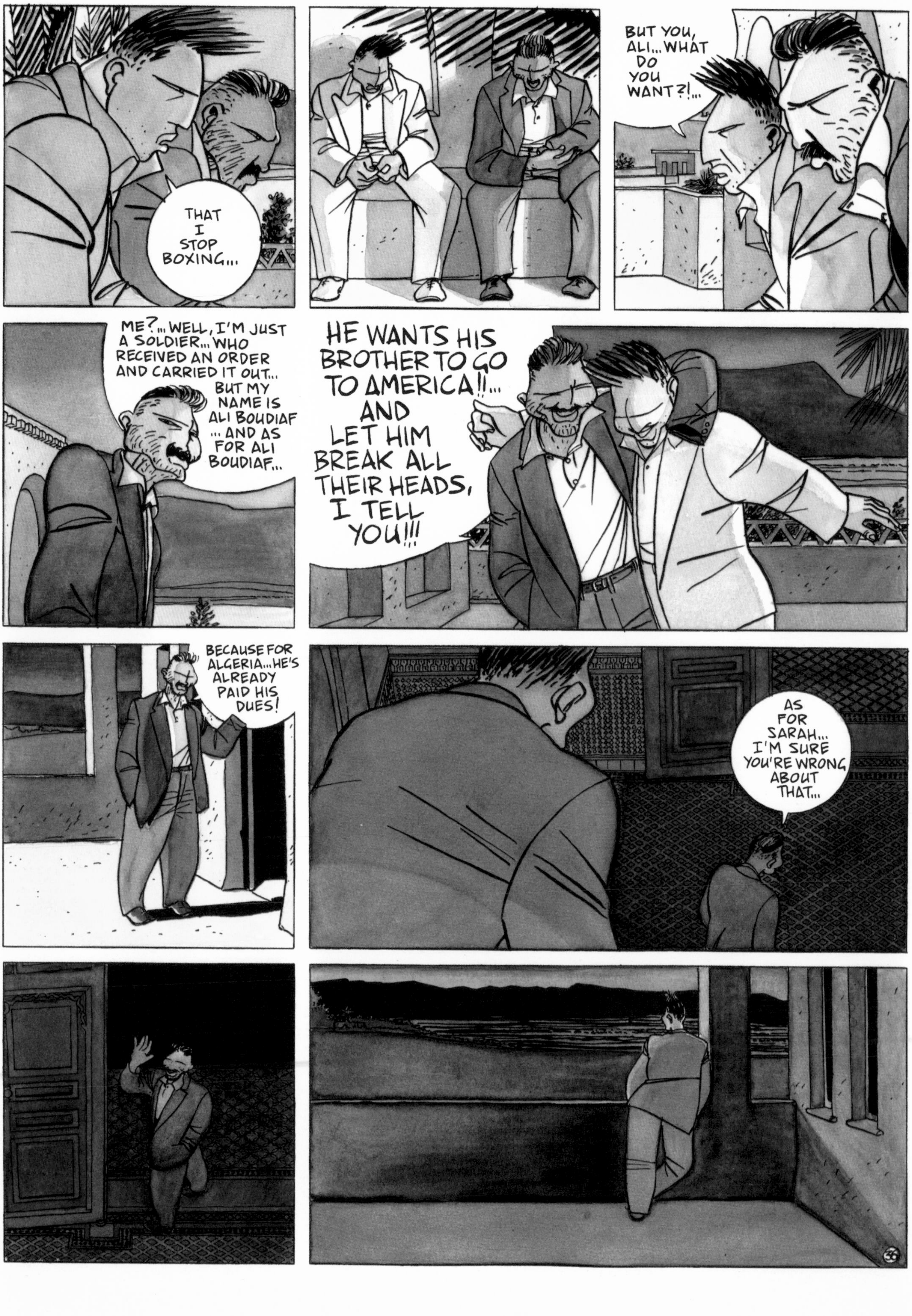
THAT I STOP BOXING...
BUT YOU, ALI... WHAT DO YOU WANT?!...
ME?... WELL, I'M JUST A SOLDIER... WHO RECEIVED AN ORDER AND CARRIED IT OUT... BUT MY NAME IS ALI BOUDIAF ...AND AS FOR ALI BOUDIAF...
HE WANTS HIS BROTHER TO GO TO AMERICA!!... AND LET HIM BREAK ALL THEIR HEADS, I TELL YOU!!!
BECAUSE FOR ALGERIA... HE'S ALREADY PAID HIS DUES!
AS FOR SARAH... I'M SURE YOU'RE WRONG ABOUT THAT...

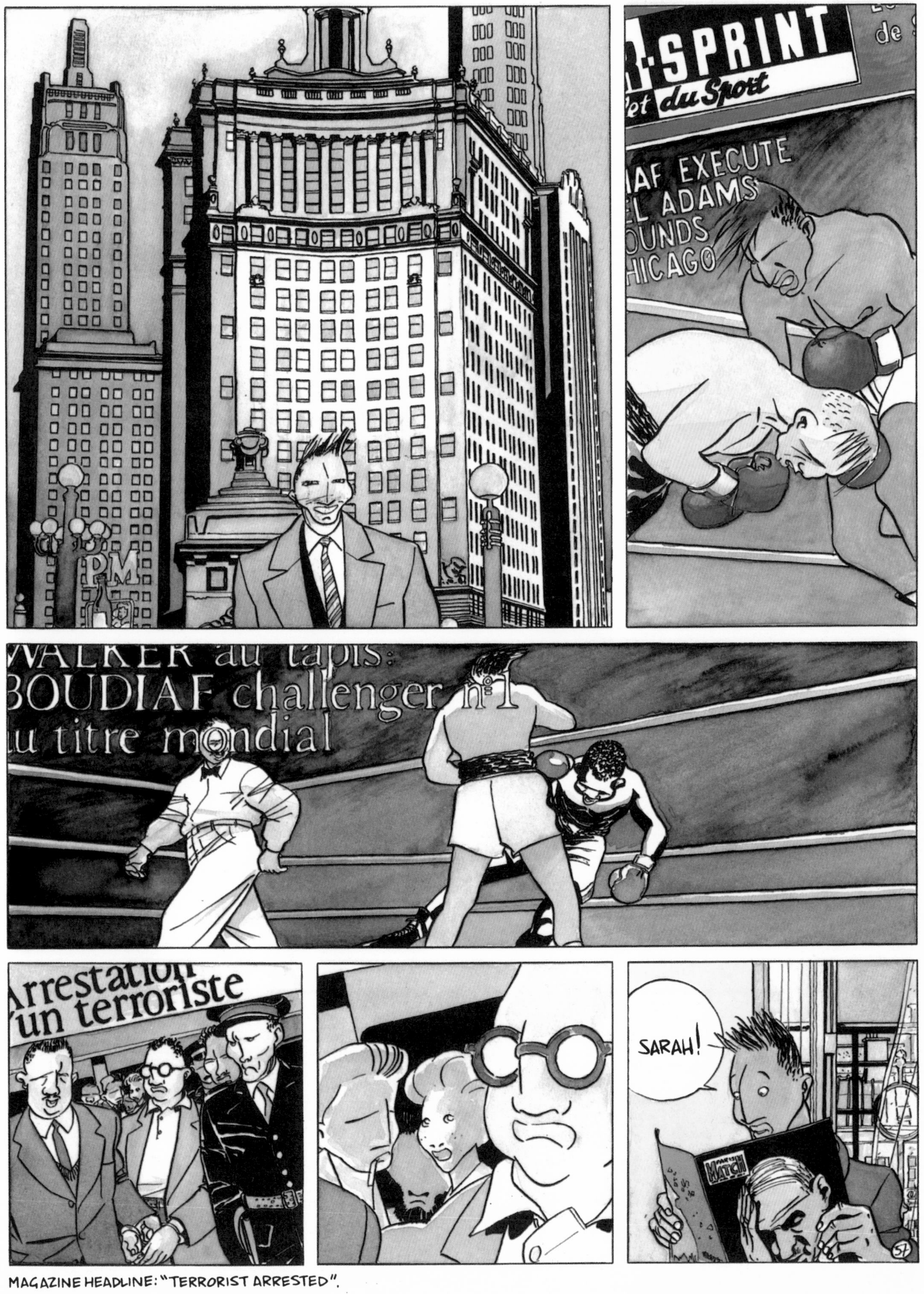
R-SPRINT
et du Sport
de S
IAF EXECUTE
EL ADAMS
OUNDS
HICAGO
VALKER au tapis:
BOUDIAF challenger n°1
u titre mondial
Arrestation
un terroriste
SARAH!
MATCH

MAGAZINE HEADLINE: "TERRORIST ARRESTED".

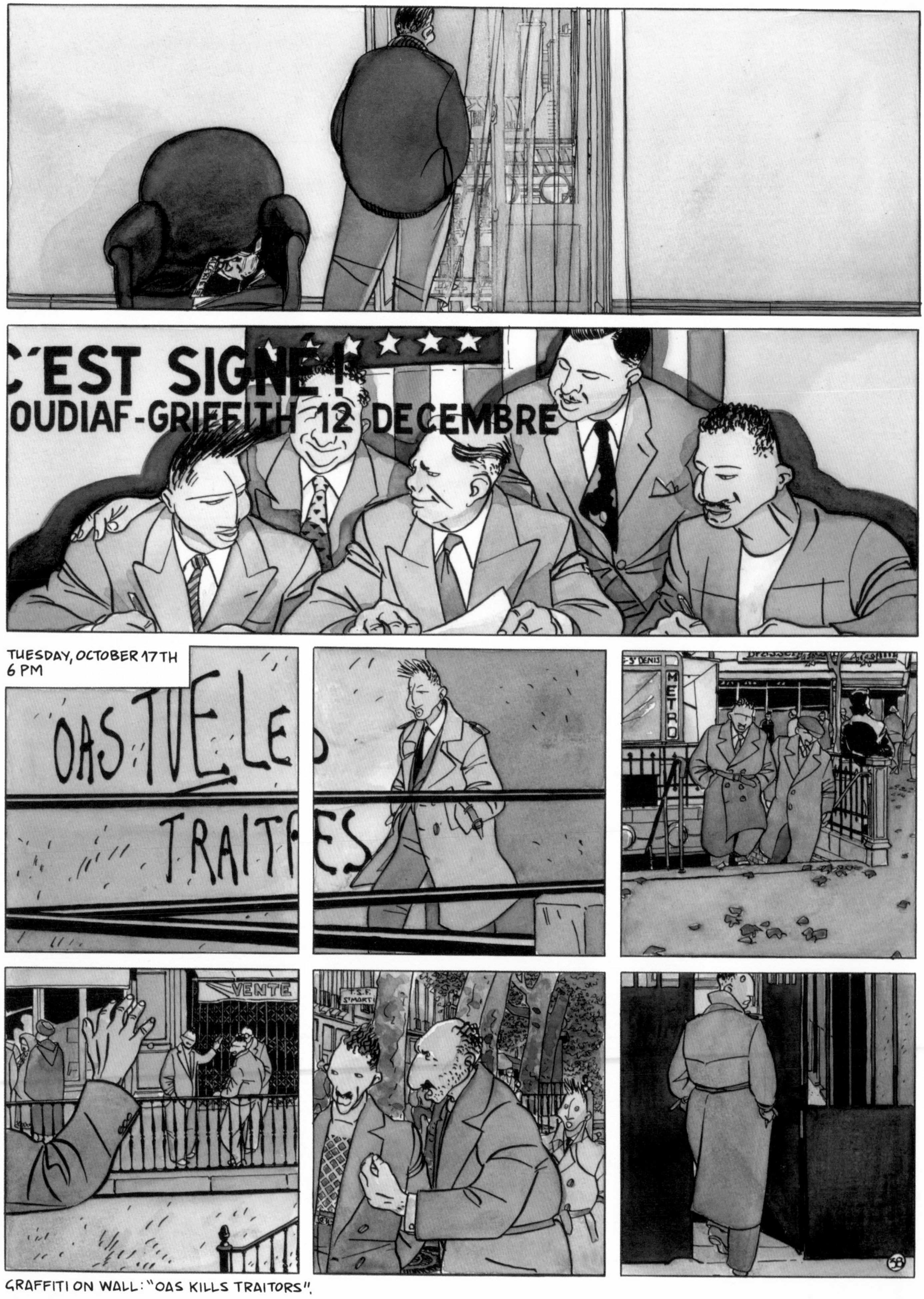
C'EST SIGNE!
OUDIAF-GRIFFITH 12 DECEMBRE
TUESDAY, OCTOBER 17TH
6 PM
OAS TUE LE
TRAIT ES
METRO
VENTE

GRAFFITI ON WALL: "OAS KILLS TRAITORS".

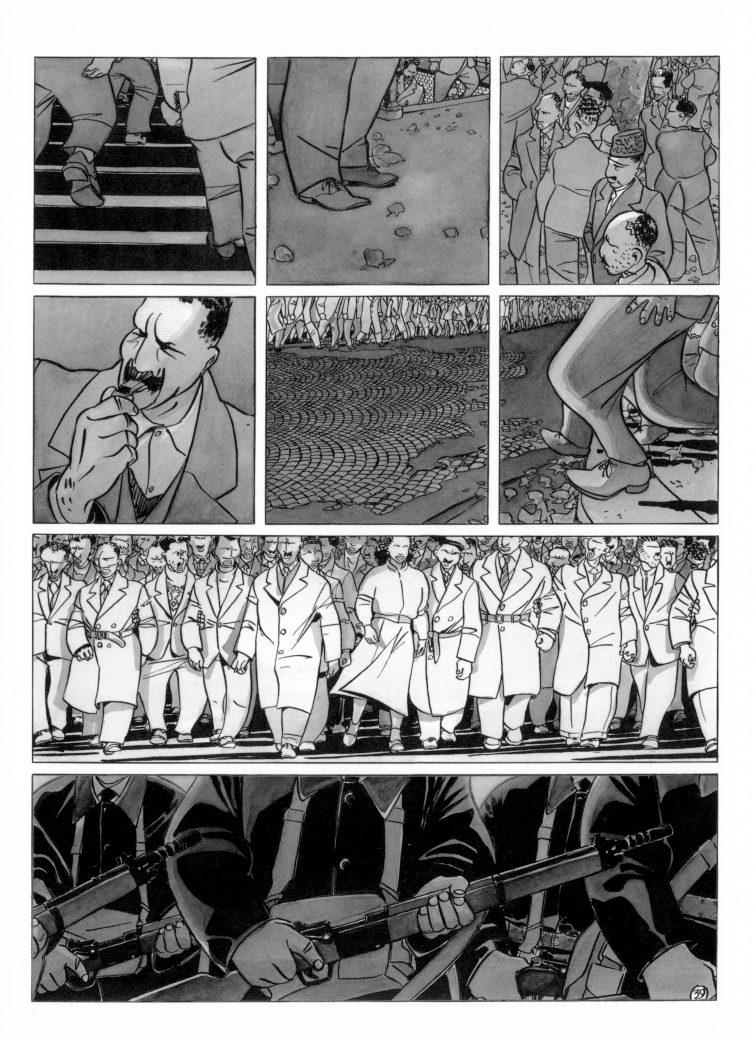

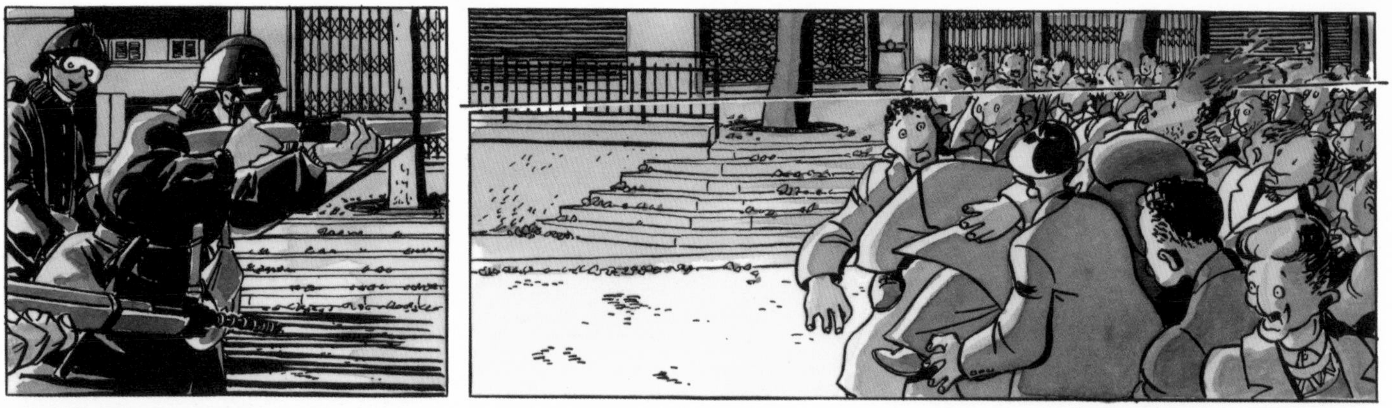

ON TUESDAY, OCTOBER 17 1961, THIRTY THOUSAND ALGERIANS TOOK TO THE STREETS OF PARIS IN PEACEFUL PROTEST AGAINST THE DISCRIMINATORY CURFEW THAT WAS IMPOSED ON THEM... AT 7:30 PM, THE POLICE CHARGED. THE ASSAULT BECAME A BLOODY FREE-FOR-ALL.

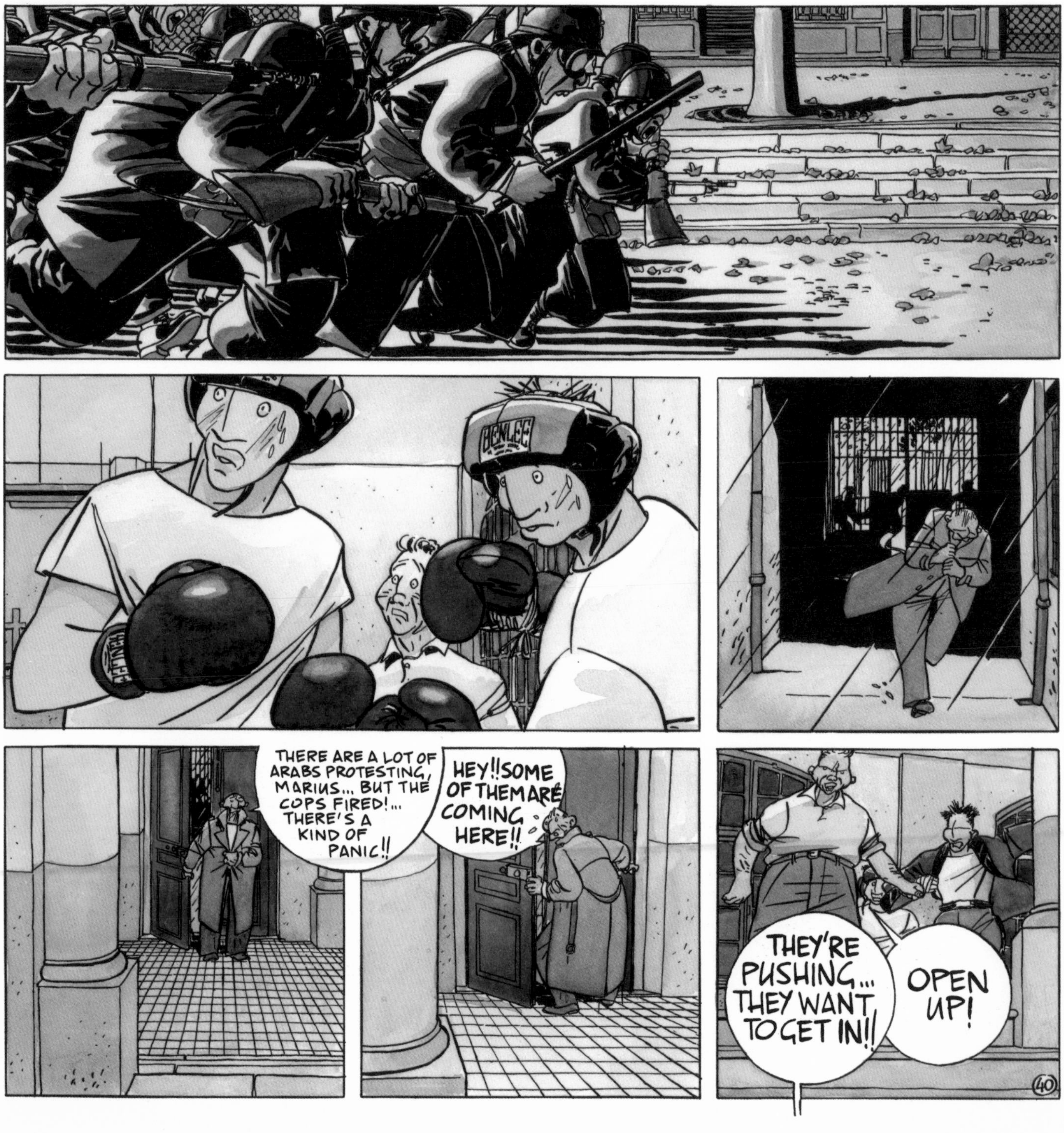
BENLEE
THERE ARE A LOT OF ARABS PROTESTING, MARIUS... BUT THE COPS FIRED!... THERE'S A KIND OF PANIC!!
HEY!! SOME OF THEM ARE COMING HERE!!
THEY'RE PUSHING... THEY WANT TO GET IN!!
OPEN UP!

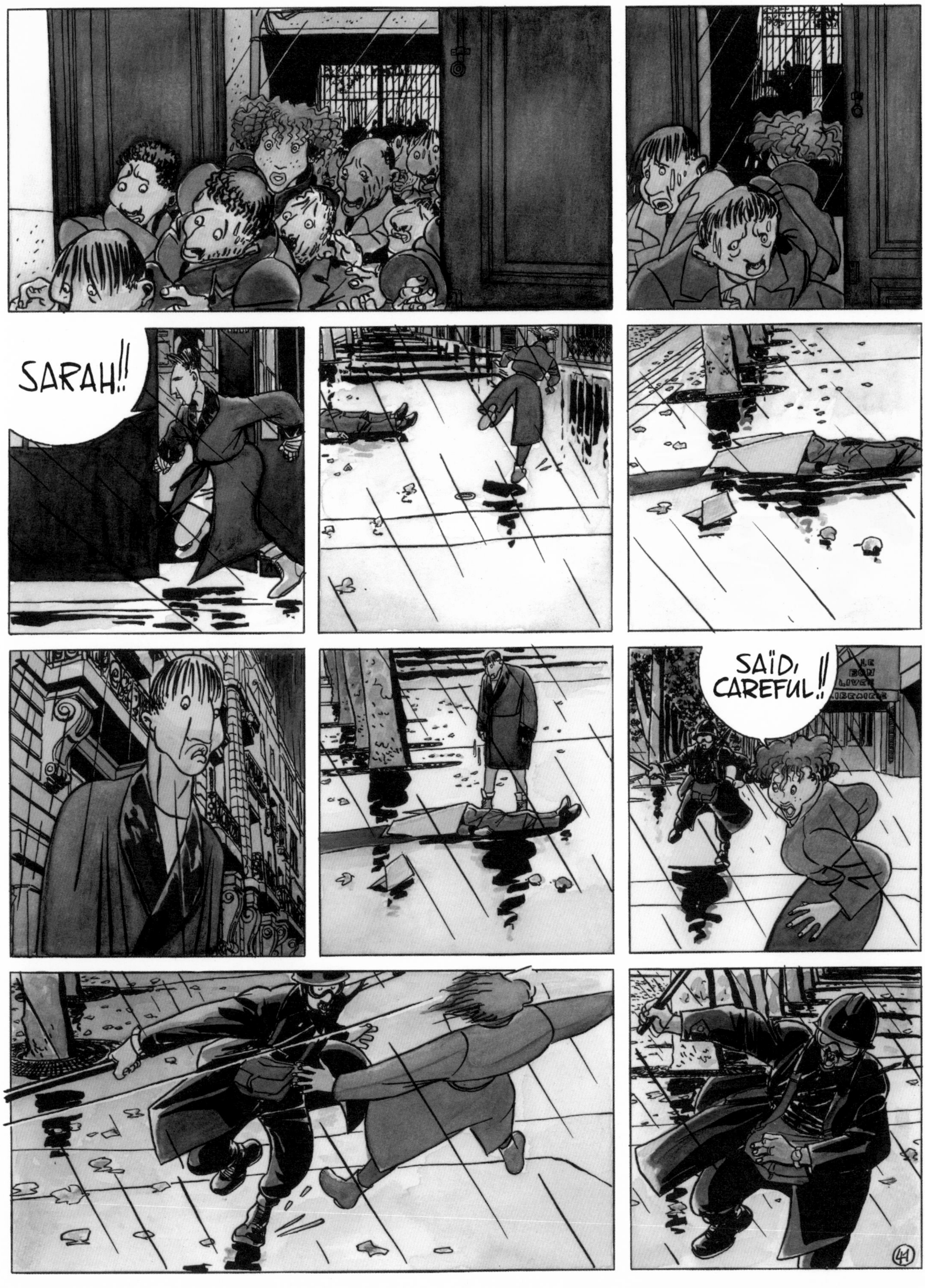
SARAH!!
SAÏD, CAREFUL!!

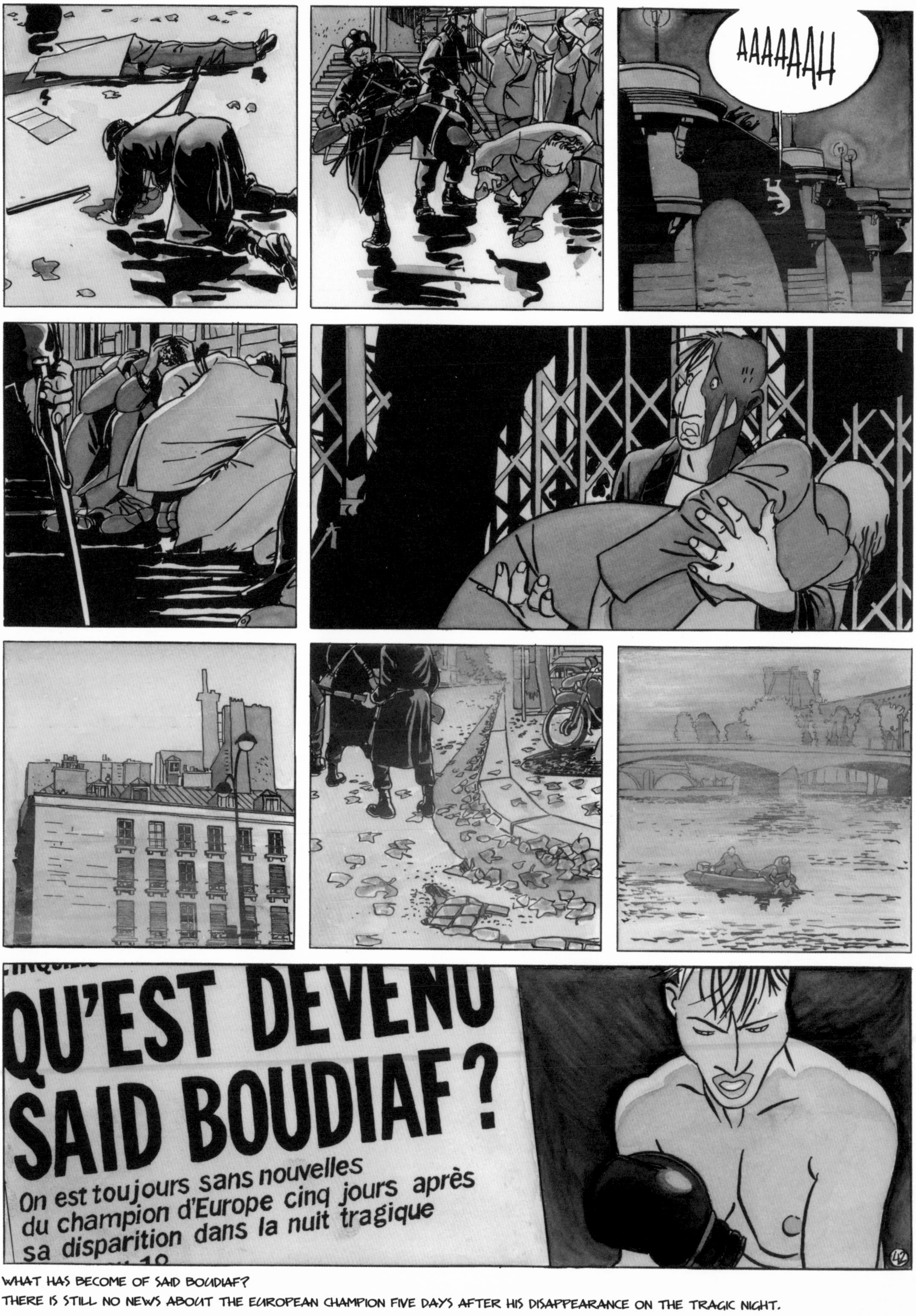
AAAAAAH
QU'EST DEVENU
SAID BOUDIAF ?
On est toujours sans nouvelles
du champion d'Europe cinq jours après
sa disparition dans la nuit tragique

WHAT HAS BECOME OF SAID BOUDIAF?
THERE IS STILL NO NEWS ABOUT THE EUROPEAN CHAMPION FIVE DAYS AFTER HIS DISAPPEARANCE ON THE TRAGIC NIGHT.

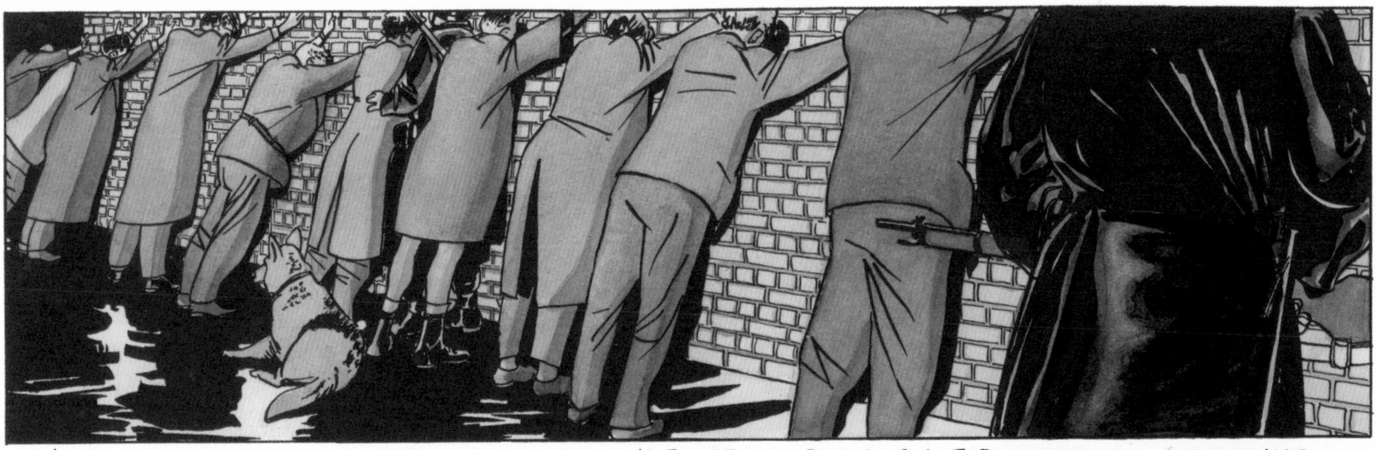

YES!... WHAT DID HAPPEN TO SAÏD BOUDIAF? WAS HE AMONG THOSE WHO DIED ON THAT TERRIBLE NIGHT IN OCTOBER '61?

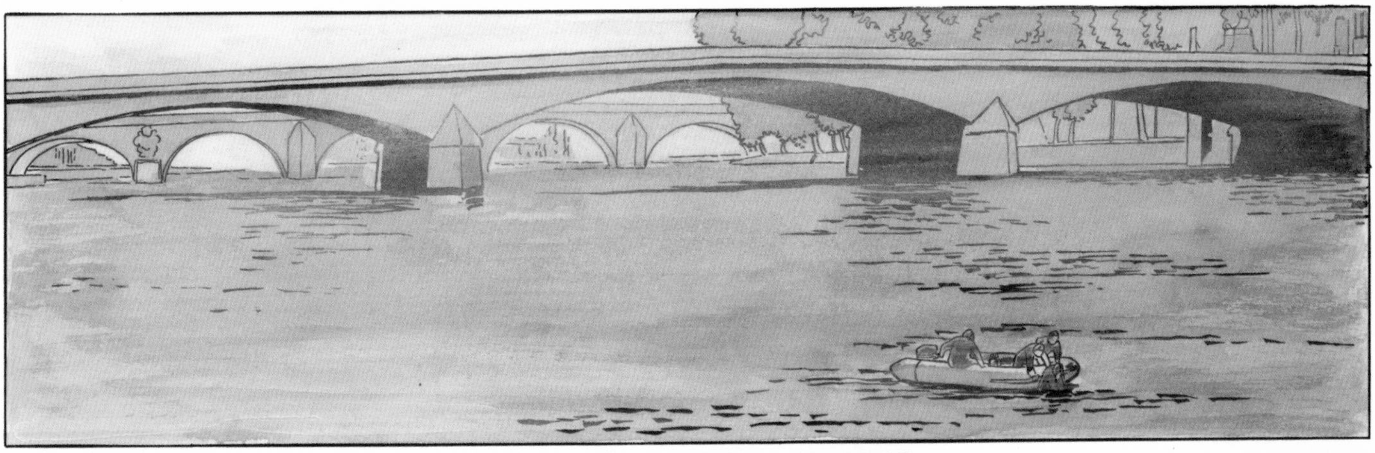

WAS HIS BODY ONE OF THOSE DRAGGED FROM THE SEINE IN THE EARLY MORNING?

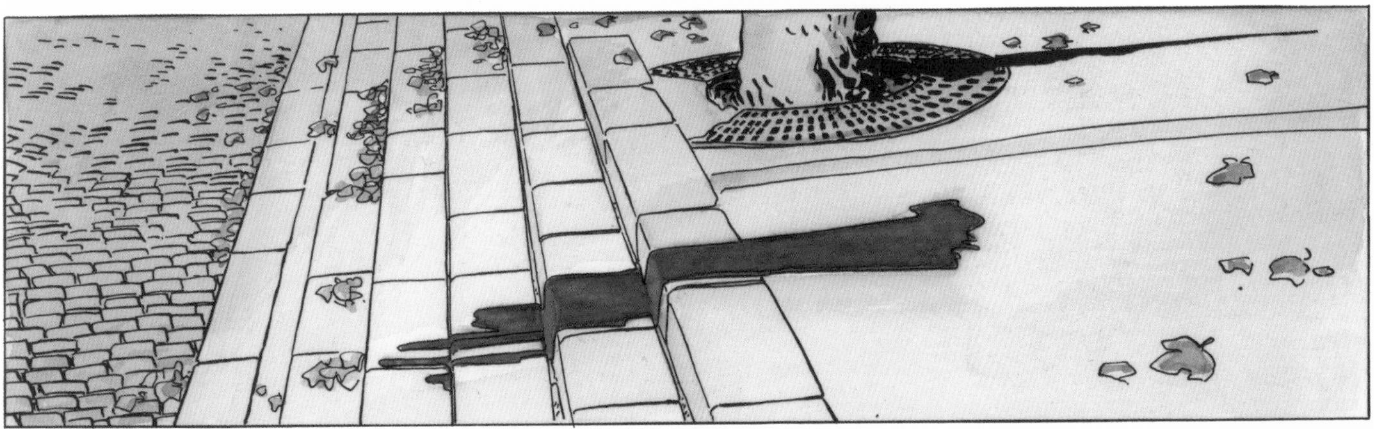

OR WAS HE DISCREETLY DISPOSED OF ALONG WITH HIS TEN (TWENTY? THIRTY? FORTY?) COMPATRIOTS WHO WERE ASSASSINATED THAT EVENING?

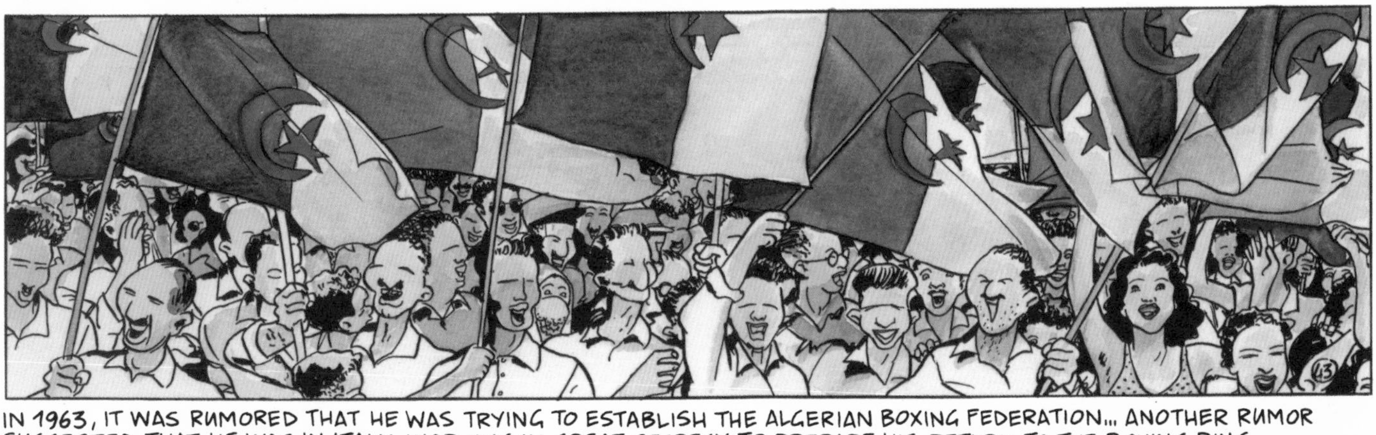

IN 1963, IT WAS RUMORED THAT HE WAS TRYING TO ESTABLISH THE ALGERIAN BOXING FEDERATION... ANOTHER RUMOR SUGGESTED THAT HE WAS IN ITALY, WORKING IN GREAT SECRECY TO PREPARE HIS RETURN TO THE BOXING RING...

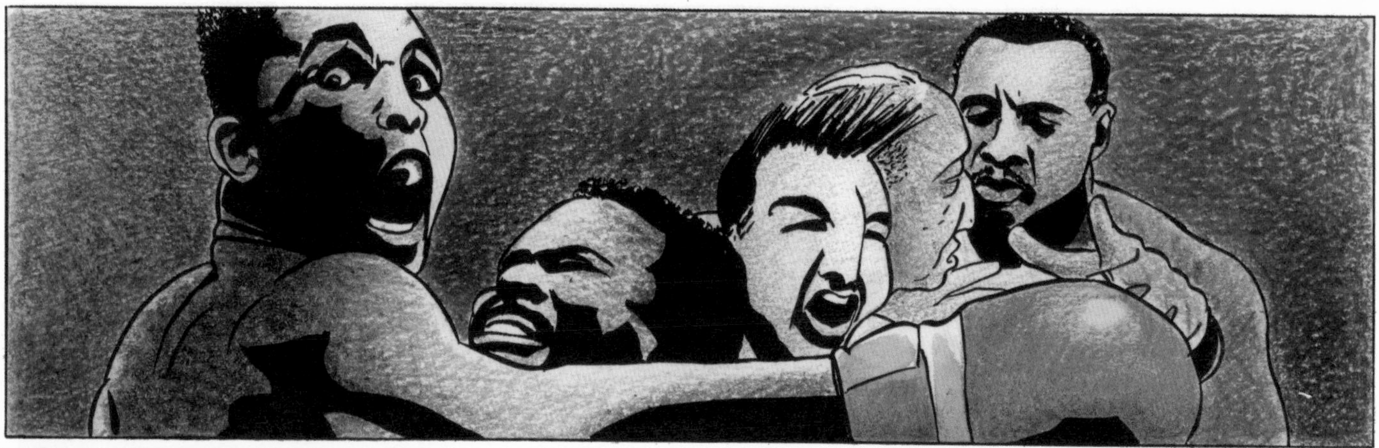

LATER, SOME CLAIMED TO SEE HIM IN THE SHADOWS OF CASSIUS CLAY'S FIRST TRIUMPHS...

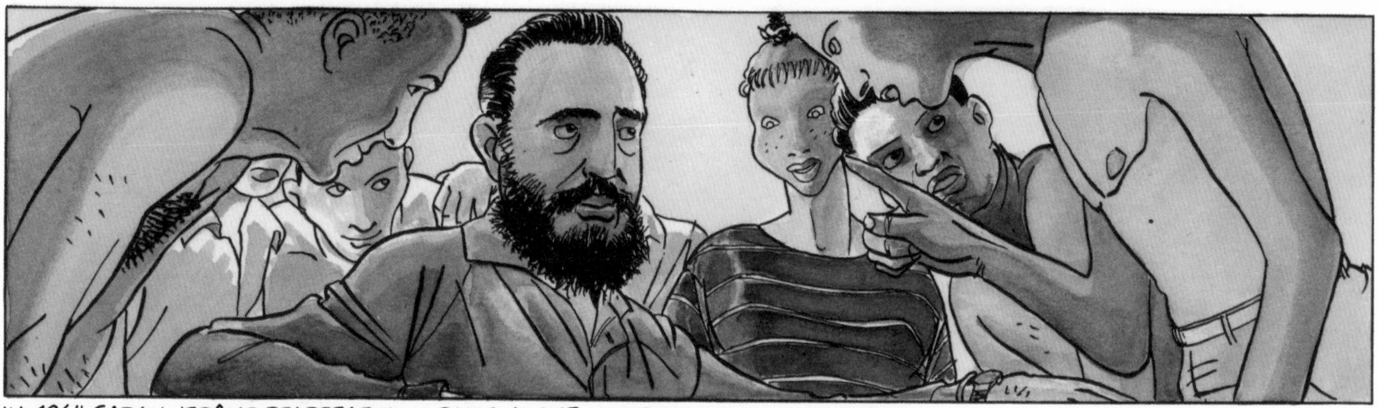

IN 1964 SARAH JERÔME REAPPEARED IN PARIS. ALONE. SHE RETREATED TO COMPLETE SILENCE. IN SEPTEMBER SHE WENT TO CUBA, TO LOSE HERSELF IN THE TUMULTUOUS MEANDERINGS OF THE CASTRO REVOLUTION.

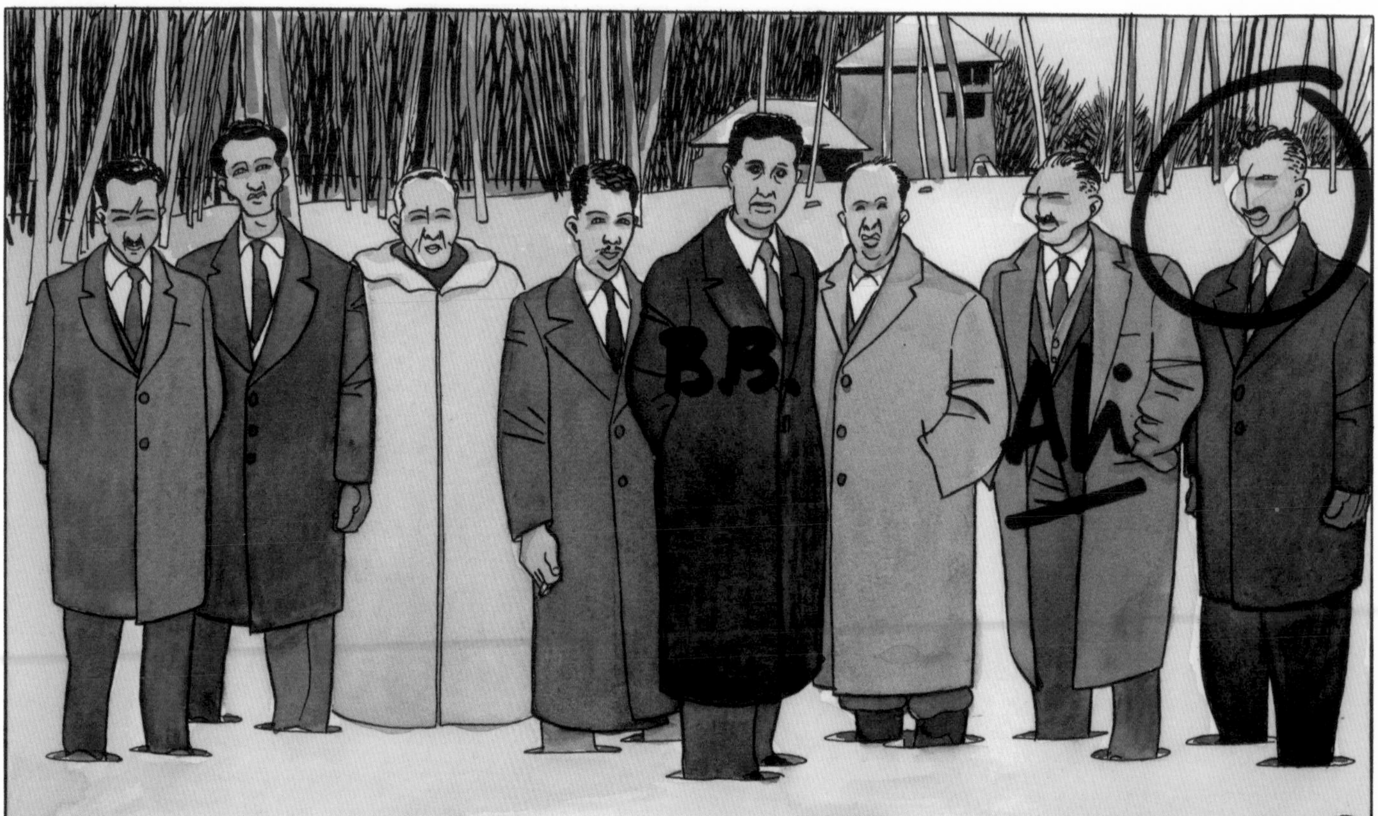
B.B.
Ali

IN 1965, COL. HOUARI BOUMEDIENNE CHASED AHMED BEN BELLA FROM POWER... A SWISS NEWSPAPER PUBLISHED A PHOTOGRAPH FROM HIS EARLY EXILE... TO THE LEFT OF THE FALLEN PRESIDENT ONE COULD RECOGNIZE ALI BOUDIAF... ALL AGREED THAT THE INDIVIDUAL AT HIS SIDE WAS NONE OTHER THAN SAÏD BOUDIAF... BUT WAS IT REALLY?

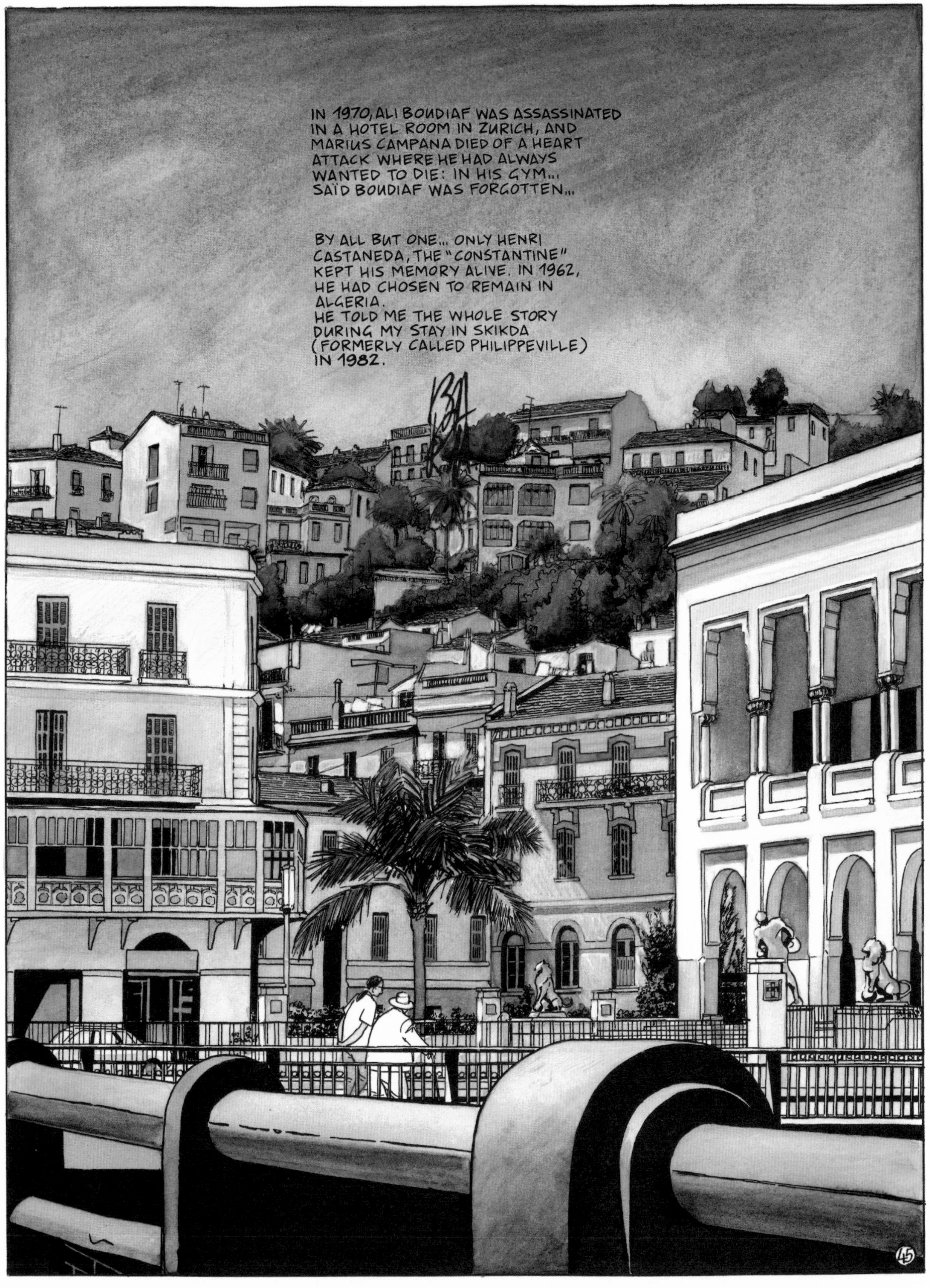
IN 1970, ALI BOUDIAF WAS ASSASSINATED IN A HOTEL ROOM IN ZURICH, AND MARIUS CAMPANA DIED OF A HEART ATTACK WHERE HE HAD ALWAYS WANTED TO DIE: IN HIS GYM... SAÏD BOUDIAF WAS FORGOTTEN...
BY ALL BUT ONE... ONLY HENRI CASTANEDA, THE "CONSTANTINE" KEPT HIS MEMORY ALIVE. IN 1962, HE HAD CHOSEN TO REMAIN IN ALGERIA. HE TOLD ME THE WHOLE STORY DURING MY STAY IN SKIKDA (FORMERLY CALLED PHILIPPEVILLE) IN 1982.

PRINTED IN ITALY